SPOOKS, SCARLETT

Sc... Enigma

by

David Dowson

TABLE OF CONTENTS

CHAPTER ONE: A MYSTERIOUS CODE NAME.

The corridors of the Secret Intelligence Service (S.I.S), buzzed with anticipation as a new case landed on the desks of its intelligent agents. This time, the case revolved around a mysterious figure named David Scarlett. The enigma surrounding Scarlett had gripped the agency, leaving them determined to unravel the secrets that shrouded his identity.

Scarlett was a name that had emerged from the shadows, captivating the attention of intelligence professionals worldwide. Despite extensive investigations and surveillance efforts, little was known about him. His presence seemed to materialize out of thin air, leaving a trail of unanswered questions in his wake. This mysterious figure had somehow managed to remain undetected, an enigmatic puzzle that needed solving.

As the case file made its way from one department to another, the atmosphere in the S.I.S headquarters became charged with anticipation. The agency's best minds pored over every detail, sifting through a multitude of reports, research, testimonies, and classified information, hoping to piece together the puzzle of David Scarletts. Their desks were littered with files, photographs, and redacted documents, forming a visual representation of their tireless efforts to uncover his true identity.

In the intelligence analysis rooms, agents gathered around large screens, displaying an intricate web of connections and leads. The buzz of conversation filled the air as theories were proposed, dissected, and debated.
Who was David Scarletts?

Was he a double agent?

A master spy?

Or perhaps a high-ranking government official operating under an alias?

The possibilities seemed endless, each one more tantalizing than the last.

Agents delved into Scarlett's' past, scrutinizing any trace of his existence. They scoured public records, financial transactions, and travel patterns, hoping to find any clue that would lead them closer to the truth. But scarlets seemed to have left no trail, his presence veiled in a carefully constructed façade.sarlets had become a matter of professional pride, a test of their intelligence-gathering capabilities.

Days turned into weeks, and weeks into months, but the identity of David Scarlett's remained elusive. However, the relentless pursuit of the truth continued unabated. The corridors of the S.I.S echoed with the hum of activity, as agents tirelessly chased leads, examined evidence, and pieced together fragments of information.

And so, the corridors of the S.I.S continued to buzz with anticipation, as the agency's agents pressed on, determined to peel back the layers of secrecy surrounding David Scarletts. They knew that the answer lay hidden somewhere, waiting to be discovered.

Agent Elizabeth Morgan, renowned for her sharp intellect and exceptional puzzle-solving skills, stood confidently before her superiors in the headquarters of the Secret Intelligence Service (S.I.S). The room was filled with high-ranking officials, all eager to discuss the handling of the perplexing case of David Scarlett's.

As the discussion began, Agent Morgan listened attentively, her gaze focused and determined. Her superiors acknowledged her reputation for unravelling complex mysteries, recognizing her as the ideal candidate to tackle the enigma that was David Scarletts. They understood the significance of her involvement in this case, knowing that her unique perspective and analytical abilities would be vital in deciphering the truth.

Agent Morgan absorbed the details of the case. Her superiors presented the limited information they had gathered about Scarletts, emphasizing the mysterious nature of his identity and the challenges that had stumped their best intelligence agents. They outlined the resources available to her, including access to classified files, surveillance equipment, and a team of trusted operatives who would assist her in the investigation.

After a moment of addressing her, they gave her the floor to discuss her findings. Before she proceeded with her findings, Agent Morgan's analytical mind immediately sprang into action.

She asked probing questions, seeking clarification and identifying any potential leads from the information they gave her that could help in uncovering Scarletts' true identity.

'That's enough now, Agent Morgan. Proceed with your findings, please,' Agent Jacko Mane said. A short-looking old agent with the toughest face in the room.

Agent Morgan activates the projector, and the first slide appears on the screen, showing a picture of David Scarletts. 'Thank you, sir. As you can see, I've compiled my findings into a slide presentation. Let's begin.'

'First and foremost, it's important to note that David Scarletts is not his real name. It is, in fact, a code name assigned to him by the intelligence community. This code name was given due to his exceptional ability to vanish without a trace, leaving little to no evidence behind.

'Can you elaborate on the reasoning behind this code name?' Agent Tola asked

'Certainly. We have discovered a pattern in Scarletts' operations through extensive research and analysis. He possesses a unique skill set that allows him to effortlessly evade capture and erase any trace of his presence. This led the intelligence community to assign him the code name "David Scarletts" as a nod to his ability to disappear like a magician. Though some would argue that he chose this name himself as he had come to refer to himself that way before the name was assigned.'

Agent Morgan clicks to the next slide, which displays a timeline of Scarletts' operations. 'This timeline showcases Scarletts' covert activities over the past decade. As you can see, he has operated under various aliases, constantly changing his identity to remain elusive. This deliberate strategy has made it incredibly difficult to trace his true origins or background.

Agent Morgan advances to the next slide, revealing a series of images showing Scarletts in different disguises.

'As part of our investigation, we managed to obtain these images, which depict Scarletts assuming different identities throughout his operations. These disguises and his knowledge of various languages and accents further support our belief that he is a master of deception. Some reports claim these are just his allies he sends out in his place.'

'It seems Scarletts has remain one step ahead for quite some time. What should be our next course of action?' Agent Jacko asked

'We need to intensify our efforts to unveil his true identity. We should focus on tracing his digital footprint, examining his financial transactions, and deepening our understanding of his network. Additionally, we should leverage our international alliances to gather any intelligence on his activities or potential associates.'

'Certainly. As you can see, we are all buzzing to get that done. Tell us something new, Agent Morgan, something we don't know. Your dedication and insight into this case has certainly been invaluable. We trust in your abilities to continue pursuing the truth behind Scarletts' identity. So you've got to have something bigger than this for us.'

'Absolutely, sir. Our investigations have revealed that David Scarletts is ed exceptionally skilled mastermind not just an elusive figure. He has a deep understanding of espionage techniques, enabling him to operate covertly and gather undetected sensitive information. His expertise in hacking and manipulation allows him to exploit vulnerabilities in digital systems and manipulate individuals to achieve his objectives.

Agent Jacko nodded absentmindedly.

'That's the enigma we're still trying to unravel, sir. Still, despite his impressive skill set, his true motives remain unknown. Our intelligence suggests that Scarletts is driven by something beyond personal gain. There are indications of his involvement in high-level geopolitical activities, but the precise nature of his secrets eludes us.

'Agent Morgan, considering his abilities and the elusive nature of his objectives, what strategies do you propose to get closer to uncovering his secrets?' Agent Tola asked. She seem to be the only one attentive as the rest of the Agents in the room look like they were sodding off.

'To approach Scarletts effectively, we need to think outside the box. Traditional investigative methods might not be sufficient in this case. I recommend utilizing a combination of technical expertise, human intelligence, and unconventional approaches. We should consider deploying a specialized team that excels in counter-espionage and cyber warfare to counter his tactics head-on.'

'Based on what you've discovered so far, do you believe Scarletts is operating alone, or is he part of a larger organization?' Agent Tola asked. 'This is not getting anywhere. She is saying what everyone is saying. We are going in cycles here.' Agent Jacko whispered to Tola, who ignored him and listened to Elizabeth.

'Well, while we haven't definitively established his affiliations, there are indications that he may be connected to a clandestine network. The complexity of his operations and the resources at his disposal suggest that he could have the backing of a sophisticated organization. However, further investigation is required to uncover the extent of these connections.

'Agent Morgan, have we made any progress in identifying Scarletts' true identity? Is there any information that might lead us closer to him?' Agent Thron finally spoke. He was the tallest man in the room. Who looked just as intimidating as Jacko. However, he looked like he had eyes that were permanently closed, though they were open, watching people quietly.

'Yes sir, we are actively pursuing every lead, but Scarlett has left a remarkably small footprint. Our analysis suggests that he possesses extensive knowledge of counterintelligence and has taken significant precautions to protect his true identity. However, we continue to investigate potential vulnerabilities, such as past associates, financial transactions, and any irregularities in his digital presence.'

Agent Jacko rolled his eyes.

'Agent Morgan, it seems we have a formidable challenge ahead of us.' Agent Thron said, rolling his pen in his hands while looking at Elizabeth through his seemingly closed eyes. 'But your insights and dedication to this case are quite simple. We need to be updated on any breakthroughs or significant developments. We're counting on your expertise.' they were about to dismiss her when Elizabeth called out

'Wait!' they all raise their heads to look at her.

recurring pattern emerged as I dug deeper into Scarletts' operations. He appears to have been involved in a series of covert operations within significant geopolitical locations. However, what sets these operations apart is that they seem to have a common theme: exposing corruption and unveiling hidden truths that powerful entities seek to conceal.

Agent Jacko raised an eyebrow, in scepticism 'Agent Morgan, are you suggesting that Scarletts is some sort of vigilante, operating outside the boundaries of the intelligence community?'

'It is a possibility, sir. The evidence I've gathered points towards Scarletts challenging the status quo and exposing corruption within influential circles. His actions seem to be driven by a strong sense of justice and a desire to shed light on the truth. While it is unconventional, his methods have been effective in revealing the hidden agendas of powerful entities.

'Agent Morgan, you must understand the implications of what you're suggesting. Scarletts' actions, regardless of their intentions, undermine the work of the intelligence community. We have been trying to track him down for years, considering him a significant threat. Are you implying that we should support his efforts?' Agent Thron asked. This voice sounded like a silent bang that sent ripples of fear through people.

'I understand the concerns, sir. Scarletts' actions do pose challenges to the established intelligence protocols and operations. However, I believe it is crucial to look beyond the surface and evaluate the larger impact of his actions. His ability to expose corruption and unveil hidden truths indicates a potential alignment with our shared objectives of maintaining global stability and justice.'

'Agent Morgan, while his intentions might seem noble, we cannot ignore the fact that Scarletts operates outside the purview of our agencies. It raises questions about his motivations and who he ultimately answers to. We must prioritize the security of our intelligence operations and prevent any further breaches caused by his actions.' Agent Jacko said sternly

'I completely understand the need to ensure our operations remain secure, sir. However, I believe there is an opportunity here to reevaluate our approach. Scarletts' actions, while unorthodox, have provided valuable insights and exposed corruption that might have otherwise remained hidden. Perhaps there is a way to channel his unique skills and knowledge towards our shared goals, while still maintaining a level of control and oversight.'

Agent Tola chuckled 'Thinking outside the box. Are we now?' Elizabeth bowed her head. 'Agent Morgan, we appreciate your perspective, but we must exercise caution. Scarletts' true motives remain unknown, and his methods are unpredictable. We cannot risk compromising ongoing operations or jeopardizing the safety of our agents by aligning ourselves with an individual who operates in the shadows.'

'Understood, ma'am. My intention is not to blindly endorse Scarletts or his actions. I merely propose that we examine the larger implications of his activities and explore avenues to work alongside him, with the necessary precautions in place. We must adapt and evolve our approach to effectively counter the challenges he poses.

'Our dedication to this case and your ability to think outside the box are commendable. We will carefully consider your insights and recommendations. However, we must proceed with caution. Scarletts remains a threat to the intelligence community until we have a clear understanding of his objectives and allegiances.' Agent Truce said.

Elizabeth was surprised to hear him talk. She had not spotted him in the room since she walked in

'Thank you, sir. I understand the gravity of the situation and the need for caution. I will continue my investigations and provide updates accordingly. Rest assured, my priority is to protect the interests of the intelligence community while striving for justice and uncovering the truth surrounding David Scarletts

They all nodded. Agent Morgan excused herself and walked out.

As Agent Elizabeth Morgan stepped out of the conference room, her mind was swirling with a mix of excitement and nervousness. The weight of the David Scarletts case was obvious, and she couldn't help but feel the immense responsibility that came with it. Breathing in and out deeply, she tried to calm her racing thoughts and focus on the task ahead.

This case was a pivotal moment in her career. Being chosen to lead the investigation was both an honour and a challenge. Despite being one of the competent agents in the S.I.S., she never expected to be entrusted with such a high-profile assignment so early on. The opportunity to prove herself and improve her reputation in the office was not only lost on her, but the success in uncovering the true identity of David Scarletts could potentially lead to the promotion she had been working towards.

Walking briskly through the bustling corridors of the S.I.S headquarters, Agent Morgan found solace in the familiarity of the environment. She had spent countless hours within these walls, honing her skills and cultivating relationships with her colleagues. Now, as she embarked on this daunting investigation, she knew that their support and collaboration was everything she needed. She couldn't afford to let her superiors down.

Entering her office, Agent Morgan took a moment to gather her thoughts. The walls were adorned with maps, evidence boards, and photographs, all meticulously arranged to help her make sense of the puzzle that was David Scarletts. Though she had just started, she was determined to make significant progress.

Sitting at her desk, Elizabeth pulled up the information gathered so far on her computer screen. She meticulously reviewed the evidence, searching for any connections or patterns that might reveal the true identity of Scarletts. Each piece of the puzzle she unearthed brought a renewed sense of certitude and excitement.

As Agent Elizabeth Morgan scrolled through her computer, she found herself plagued by conflicting thoughts. Flashbacks of her findings and the enigmatic nature of Scarlett's activities played like a reel in her mind.

Scarlett was an impressive figure, someone who operated in the realm of black and white without being tainted by shades of grey. His skillset and the activities of his team had greatly undermined the works of the intelligence community. They were involved in high-level espionage operations that seemed to elude the grasp of even the most skilled operatives.

But amidst the chaos and uncertainty, Elizabeth couldn't help but recognize that there was an underlying sense of purpose in Scarlett's actions. Despite the disruption he caused, his activities seemed to align with causes related to justice, human rights, and the exposure of illicit activities. It was as if he was fighting a shadow war against powerful entities that manipulated and controlled society.

Elizabeth recalled instances where Scarlett's operations had brought down corrupt politicians, exposed human rights violations, and dismantled criminal organizations. His targets were often individuals and entities that had evaded justice through their power and influence. He seemed to be a champion for the marginalized and voiceless, using his skills to level the playing field.

She couldn't deny that there was a certain allure to Scarlett's actions. The intelligence community, despite its noble intentions, sometimes found itself limited by bureaucracy and politics. Scarlett, on the other hand, operated outside these confines, unburdened by red tape and able to strike at the heart of corruption with precision and anonymity.

But as alluring as his actions may have been, Elizabeth understood the delicate balance that needed to be maintained. The intelligence community existed to protect national security and maintain stability. Scarletts' activities, however noble their intentions may seem, disrupted the established order and put ongoing operations at risk.

The intelligence community had spent years, if not decades, attempting to track down Scarlett and bring him to justice. They viewed him as a threat to their very existence, a renegade force that operated beyond their control. They were committed to upholding the rule of law and protecting the interests of the nation, and viewed Scarlett as a destabilizing force.

Elizabeth had to remind herself of the potential consequences of Scarlett's actions. His operations, while seemingly just, had the potential to unleash chaos and retribution. Exposing powerful entities and uncovering their illicit activities could have far-reaching consequences that extended beyond justice and into the realms of political and social upheaval.

She knew that her duty as an intelligence officer was to maintain the delicate balance between justice and stability. It was not her place to decide who deserved exposure and who deserved protection. Her role was to gather intelligence, analyze the information, and act within the confines of the law to protect the interests of the nation.

She knew that her fascination with Scarlett's actions should not cloud her judgment or lead her down a path of moral ambiguity. She had to remain focused on her mission to uncover his true identity and bring him to justice, adhering to the principles and values she swore to uphold.

She closed her eyes, taking a deep breath to steady her thoughts, Agent Morgan reaffirmed her commitment to the intelligence community and the pursuit of truth. David Scarlett may be a formidable opponent, but she would not be swayed by his allure. She would remain steadfast, uncovering who this mysterious figure is.

Elizabeth Morgan opened her eyes and found Joshua, her trusted secretary, engrossed in organizing files and meticulously arranging documents on her desk. Joshua, a geekishly handsome man with his glasses perched on his nose, looked up from his work as he sensed her presence.

'How did you get in here' Elizabeth asked, almost startled.

Joshua smiled warmly and replied, 'Good morning, Agent Elizabeth Morgan. How did the meeting with the superiors go?'

Elizabeth returned the smile 'Good morning, Joshua. The meeting was intense, to say the least.

'Well, well, Agent Morgan, back from the lion's den, I see.'

Elizabeth chuckled 'Seems everyone already knows what we know.'

Joshua had been her secretary since she joined the agency, and his unwavering support had become an invaluable asset to her. His attention to detail and protective nature towards Elizabeth was also well-known in the office.

'The superiors were their usual sceptical selves, but I managed to hold my ground. David Scarlett has them on their toes, that's for sure.'

Joshua is an average-height man with a beard. His rugged appearance and unique style made him easily recognizable in a crowd. His beard, well-groomed and neatly trimmed, added a touch of character to his face.

But it was Joshua's distinctive silver-rimmed glasses that drew attention. They framed his bright blue eyes, which sparkled with intelligence and curiosity. Behind those lenses, his eyes seemed to hold a depth of knowledge and a hint of mischief.

One notable feature of Joshua's face was his nearly non-existent lips, concealed by the abundance of facial hair. It was only when he spoke that people realized he had lips, as they appeared slightly thin and were often overshadowed by his beard. However, when he opened his mouth, his words flowed with eloquence and wit.

The beard, especially concentrated on his chin, amplified his almost nonexistent jawline, adding a rugged charm to his appearance. The facial hair accentuated his angular features and gave him an air of casual confidence. Despite not conforming to conventional standards of beauty, there was an undeniable attractiveness to Joshua's slightly handsome, average Joe demeanour.

His fashion sense matched his unique style. Joshua often sported a combination of casual and geeky attire, wearing plaid shirts paired with suspenders or graphic tees featuring references to pop culture. His choice of clothing reflected his personality—quirky, approachable, and unapologetically himself.

Although not conventionally striking, Joshua's physical features carried a magnetism that drew people to him. His bright blue eyes, the way his beard framed his face, and his distinctive glasses created a memorable image. But it was his warm smile, quick wit, and unwavering loyalty that truly made him stand out.

'I hope you're ready for some exciting news.' Joshua said, catching Elizabeth's attention. We've been working tirelessly to prepare for your departure to London tomorrow. The department has spared no effort in ensuring you have everything you'll need to track down David Scarlett.'

'That's great to hear, Joshua' Elizabeth felt a mix of anticipation and nervousness at the prospect of finally embarking on this crucial mission. These next steps could be pivotal in uncovering the truth behind Scarlett's elusive identity.

Joshua placed the files on her desk, carefully arranging them in a neat stack.

'Here are the necessary documents you'll need for your journey. It includes your travel itinerary, identification papers, and mission briefing. Everything has been cross-checked and verified for accuracy.' 'Joshua said, pointing to the files.

Elizabeth flipped through the documents, taking note of the meticulous attention to detail. The information was presented clearly, leaving no room for confusion or oversight.

'Quite an organization you have here.' Elizabeth said as she smiled at Joshua, impressed

Joshua beamed with pride, his eyes twinkling behind his silver-rimmed glasses. 'Thank you, Agent Morgan. It's my duty to make sure you have all the necessary tools to succeed. But that's not all. We've also made some exciting technological advancements to aid you in your mission.'

Elizabeth leaned back in her chair, eager to hear more about the technological advancements that awaited her. 'Tell me more, Joshua. What do you have in store for me?'

Joshua reached into his bag and pulled out a sleek, state-of-the-art smartphone and a compact laptop, placing them gently on the desk.

'We've equipped you with the latest communication devices. This smartphone comes with encrypted messaging capabilities, secure access to classified databases, and real-time tracking functionalities. And this laptop contains all the necessary software and programs for your intelligence analysis and field reporting.' Joshua said, grinning.

Agent Morgan picked up the smartphone, feeling the weight of its significance in her palm. She marvelled at its sleek design, knowing that beneath its polished exterior lay just the right powerful tool she needs to track down David Scarlett

'This is impressive, Joshua.'

Joshua nodded, his eyes shining with pride.

'We've spared no expense in ensuring your safety and effectiveness, Agent Morgan. We understand the gravity of this mission and the importance of your success. The department believes in your abilities, and we want to provide you with every advantage possible.'

'Thank you, Joshua.' Elizabeth said with a smile.

'I have no doubt that you will succeed, Agent Morgan.' Joshua said. For a moment, his proud smile seem to vanish as he drew closer to Elizabeth.

'Elizabeth, there's something I need to tell you before you embark on this mission.' Elizabeth lifted her eyes from the device to look at Joshua.

Joshua hesitated for a moment before deciding to share a crucial piece of information with Agent Elizabeth Morgan. Still, he knew that transparency was essential, even if it added a layer of pressure to an already significant mission. Besides, he already had Elizabeth's attention and needed to spill out whatever he had to say.

'The department believes that David Scarlett poses a significant threat, and they're not leaving this case in the hands of just one agent.' Joshua said.

Elizabeth raised an eyebrow, her curiosity piqued. 'What do you mean, Joshua? Are they assigning another agent to work apart from me?'

Joshua nodded, his expression serious yet compassionate.

'Yes, Elizabeth. The department has decided to bring in Agent Emily Martinez as an additional asset in tracking down David Scarlett. They believe that having more competent agents working will increase the chances of success. They have set a deadline Elizabeth, and if they feel you haven't made significant progress by then, they will consider replacing you with Agent Martinez.

Elizabeth felt a mix of emotions swirling within her. On one hand, she understood the reasoning behind the department's decision. David Scarlett was no ordinary target, and his actions had far-reaching consequences, there it's understandable to have one more agent on the case. However, the thought of being replaced added a weight of pressure to her already burdened shoulders.

Besides, Elizabeth was not sure she knew Agent Martinez. There were so many agents in the department that she could hardly catch up with or get to know.

'What makes her so formidable?' Elizabeth asked out loud

Joshua's expression turned serious. 'Elizabeth, Emily Martinez is an exceptional agent. She is known for her resourcefulness and tenacity. She has a proven track record of successfully closing high-profile cases. Her capabilities and determination are respected within the department. If it comes to a point where they believe she can achieve what you haven't, they won't hesitate to make the switch'

Elizabeth couldn't deny the weight of Joshua's words. The thought of someone else taking over her mission and potentially overshadowing her efforts was disconcerting.

'I understand the department's need to ensure the case is handled effectively. I don't want to be replaced, especially when I've just begun. I need to make substantial progress and prove my worth.' Elizabeth said, looking out the window.

'That's the spirit, Elizabeth. Use this as motivation to push harder and show them what you're capable of. You have unique skills and insights that brought you to this point. Trust in yourself and stay focused on the task at hand.

Elizabeth nodded, determined to prove that she was the right agent for the job. She couldn't let fear or uncertainty consume her.

'Thank you, Joshua. I'll do everything I can to ensure that Emily Martinez remains a backup plan rather than a replacement.'

Elizabeth felt a renewed sense of determination wash over her. She knew that the road ahead would be challenging, but she was ready to face it head-on. She knew that the presence of Agent Emily Martinez added an additional layer of pressure, but she was resolved to prove herself and make a significant breakthrough in the case. This mission was her opportunity to solidify her reputation within the department and showcase her competence as an agent, and this was one opportunity she does not intend to blow up.

CHAPTER TWO: FACT OR FICTION

Elizabeth Morgan stepped out of the airport on the streets of London with her small briefcase. She was immediately captivated by the kaleidoscope of sights and sounds that greeted her.

The city's architecture stood as a testament to its rich heritage and modernity. Towering landmarks, such as the iconic Big Ben, stood proudly against the skyline, their grandeur leaving a lasting impression. The Gothic spires of Westminster Abbey and the majestic dome of St. Paul's Cathedral added to the city's architectural marvels. The juxtaposition of ancient and modern was evident in the glass facades of skyscrapers like The Shard, which reached skyward, offering breathtaking views of the sprawling metropolis.

As Elizabeth navigated the streets, she noticed the diverse array of people that populated the city. Business professionals in sleek suits hurried past, their determined expressions reflecting the city's fast-paced nature. Tourists with cameras in hand marvelled at the city's landmarks, their eyes wide with wonder. Street performers entertained passersby, showcasing their talents amidst the throngs of people.

As Elizabeth walked on, she made her way to the familiar building, and a sense of nostalgia washed over her. London had always held a special place in her heart, evoking memories of her visits to her grandmother's house.

The scent of Earl Grey tea and freshly baked scones seemed to linger in the air, reminding Elizabeth of the warm and welcoming atmosphere of her grandmother's home. The memories of sitting by the fireplace, engrossed in her grandmother's captivating stories, flooded her mind.

But now, Elizabeth's purpose in London was far different. She was here on a mission, a quest to unravel the enigma that was David Scarlett. She pushed open the doors of the headquarters, greeted by the familiar hum of activity that filled the air.

London, with its vast historical archives and extensive intelligence network, held the potential for significant breakthroughs. Elizabeth knew that her determination and meticulous attention to detail, made her an invaluable asset in this mission. She knew that she had to leverage every resource available to her to uncover the truth.

As Elizabeth stepped into the S.I.S headquarters, she was greeted by fellow operatives who recognized her presence. The interior of the building exuded an air of sophistication and secrecy. The polished marble floors and elegant décor added a touch of grandeur, while the discreet surveillance cameras hinted at the security measures in place. Elizabeth made her way to the research department, where rows of computers and shelves lined with reference materials awaited her.

The familiar surroundings brought her a sense of comfort. The hum of conversations, the tapping of keyboards, and the occasional ringing of telephones filled the room. Elizabeth's focus sharpened as she walked across the room

She noticed her fellow operative's eyes briefly lingered on her, taking in her professional and elegant attire. The dark female suit she wore hugged her figure with precision, exuding confidence and sophistication.

Her choice of outfit, a long-fitted shirt with a daringly long slit, added a touch of modernity to the classic ensemble. It showcased her sense of style and hinted at her bold and assertive nature. Elizabeth's short wavy brown hair framed her face, emphasising her features and drawing attention to her piercing, deep green eyes, which sparkled with determination.

As she walked through the corridors, Elizabeth couldn't help but notice the subtle glances and nods of recognition from her colleagues. Her striking appearance, combined with her reputation as a competent agent, seemed to draw a certain level of attention, and she found herself enjoying the acknowledgement.

However, Elizabeth's focus remained unwavering. She was determined to prove herself through her skills and dedication beyond relying solely on her physical appearance. She was aware that her attractiveness could be a double-edged sword, sometimes leading to assumptions and underestimations. But she had always embraced her femininity as a source of strength, using it to her advantage in the male-dominated world of intelligence.

The attention she received as she walked through the building served as a reminder of the challenges she had overcome and the respect she had earned. It fueled her motivation to excel in this new mission and prove that she was more than just a captivating presence.

Elizabeth's journey was not just about her physical attributes; it was about her intellect, strategic thinking, and ability to adapt. She knew that her success in this one would be determined by her skills, knowledge, and determination, rather than her appearance alone.

As she made her way to her workspace, Elizabeth's demeanour remained focused and composed. She acknowledged the nods and greetings from her colleagues with a polite smile, appreciating the camaraderie within the intelligence community.

While she appreciated the attention her physical appearance brought, Elizabeth knew that it was her competence and dedication that would ultimately define her reputation within the S.I.S. And so, with a firm resolve, she embraced her role as an agent, ready to face the challenges that lay ahead and make her mark in the world of intelligence.

As Elizabeth entered the extensive MI6 archives, a sense of anticipation and excitement filled the air. Rows upon rows of shelves lined with meticulously labelled boxes and files stretched out before her, holding the secrets of countless operations and agents.

She approached Tuesday, the archivist stationed at the entrance, a knowledgeable individual who had spent years organising and cataloguing the wealth of information contained within these walls. With a polite smile, Elizabeth requested access to the files pertaining to David Scarlett's alleged connection to the British police force.

Tuesday, a seasoned professional with a penchant for details, took note of her request and led her through the labyrinthine corridors of the archives. The air was imbued with the faint scent of old paper and ink.

Finally, they arrived at a section dedicated to past operations and personnel records. Elizabeth's eyes scanned the labels on the shelves, searching for any indication of David Scarlett's involvement in the police force. She had gathered some tangible information that David Scarlett had once served in the police force in London. By tangible, this was more of disjointed rumours in the department.

Her fingers brushed against the worn spines of files, each representing a piece of history waiting to be unravelled.

With a surge of anticipation, she selected a box marked "Undercover Operations – British Police Force." The archivist provided her with gloves to handle the delicate documents.

Elizabeth carefully opened the file, revealing a treasure trove of information. She meticulously examined each document, scrutinising reports, photographs, and testimonies. The hours slipped away as she pieced together fragments of David Scarlett's past, seeking confirmation of the rumours that had brought her to this archive.

The files spoke of a skilled operative who had infiltrated criminal organisations with astonishing precision. Reports highlighted his ability to blend seamlessly into various roles, assuming different identities to gather crucial intelligence. Elizabeth's eyes widened as she read testimonies of colleagues who marvelled at his intellect, resourcefulness, and unwavering dedication to justice.

A photograph caught her attention—a young man with a chiselled jawline and piercing eyes stared back at her. The name written there was Finnan Gregory. But Elizabeth believed this to be David Scarlett, or at least one of the identities he had assumed during his time in the police force. His gaze seemed to hold a sense of purpose and determination, leaving Elizabeth with an unshakeable impression of the enigmatic figure she was pursuing.

Elizabeth discovered records of several significant operations where David Scarlett's influence had left an indelible mark on the British police force. His ability to operate under the radar, his talent for gathering crucial evidence, and his unwavering determination to expose hidden agendas had earned him the respect of his colleagues and the ire of those he sought to unveil.

As she delved deeper into the files, Elizabeth unearthed a trail of covert operations, each exposing corruption, unveiling hidden truths, and bringing down powerful entities that sought to conceal their illicit activities.

As Elizabeth closed the last file, a sense of awe and respect washed over her. David Scarlett's journey from an undercover operative in the police force to an elusive mastermind operating on a global scale unfolded before her eyes. She couldn't help but feel a mix of admiration and determination to uncover the truth behind his current activities and the enigma that surrounded him.

Still, David Scarlett's actions remained foggy and unclear. At some point, he seem to be trailed to the Soviet Union. Some files claimed he was assassinated, poisoned by the associates. It became quite overwhelming and exhausting for her as she tried to piece these strings of different information together into a whole logical piece.

Due to the weight of exhaustion, Elizabeth's mind briefly drifted away from the task at hand as memories of her grandmother, affectionately known as Nana, flooded her thoughts. She pictured her grandmother's warm smile, the twinkle in her eyes, and the comforting embrace that always made her feel safe and loved.

London had always held a special place in Elizabeth's heart, not only because of her childhood memories in London, but also because it was the city where her grandmother resided. The thought of Nana brought a sense of nostalgia and longing, prompting Elizabeth to reminisce about their special bond.

She remembered the countless visits to her grandmother's house, nestled in a quaint neighbourhood that exuded charm and history. The familiar scent of freshly brewed tea and homemade pastries wafted through the air, instantly transporting her back to the cherished moments they had shared.

Elizabeth could almost taste the delicate flavours of her grandmother's famous scones, still warm from the oven, and the soothing sensation of sipping tea from fine china cups. Nana's house was a haven, filled with cherished family heirlooms, photographs capturing precious memories, and shelves lined with books that had been passed down through generations.

The thought of seeing Nana, even for a brief moment, tugged at Elizabeth's heartstrings. It had been too long since their last meeting, and she longed for the familiar embrace that felt like a soothing balm to her weary soul.

However, Elizabeth knew that her current mission demanded her undivided attention with a deep breath, Elizabeth refocused her attention on the files spread out before her. She gently pushed aside the sentimental thoughts of her grandmother and immersed herself once again in the task at hand.

Each file held a piece of the puzzle, shedding light on David Scarlett's past and his involvement in covert operations. The weight of responsibility settled on Elizabeth's shoulders as she recognized the significance of her role in uncovering the truth.

While Elizabeth longed for a moment of respite and the comfort of her grandmother's embrace, her mind momentarily shifted to Agent Emily Martinez, a name she had heard in passing but had not paid much attention to until now. The mention of Emily potentially taking her place in the mission had ignited a flicker of curiosity and a sense of cautious intrigue within Elizabeth.

While Elizabeth was not one to easily feel threatened by others encroaching on her territory, Joshua's warning had struck a chord. It reminded her that the intelligence community operated in a competitive environment, where reputation and results held significant weight. This case involving David Scarlett was an opportunity for Elizabeth to prove herself and solidify her position within the agency.

The thought of her late father wandered into her mind alongside this thought. He was a man who had believed in her potential and greatness. He had instilled in her a sense of ambition and the drive to make a difference in the world. Elizabeth knew that seizing this chance to uncover the truth about David Scarlett could not only enhance her reputation within the agency but also fulfil the promise she had made to her father.

Determination filled her veins again. It was as if the thought of her father filled her with so much strength. She knew that her success in unravelling the mysteries surrounding David Scarlett would not only validate her abilities as an agent but also open doors to further opportunities and advancement within the intelligence community, but this was a gift to her dad. A gift that would make him lift her up in excitement and dance with her while he still held her to his arm.

The thought of that filled her with so much warmth and made her smile. Elizabeth refocused her attention on the task at hand. She meticulously reviewed the files, cross-referencing information and connecting dots to paint a clearer picture of the enigmatic figure known as David Scarlett.

But, at this point, Elizabeth realised it was much more than her exhaustion. The nature of the information before her seems to be deliberately chaotic.

The reports were disjointed, filled with conflicting accounts and fragmented details that made it difficult to discern fact from fiction. It was as if the individuals who had submitted the files were themselves unsure of the truth about David Scarlett.

She skimmed through the various reports again, noting the inconsistencies and contradictory narratives. Some sources painted David as a mastermind, a cunning manipulator who operated in the shadows, while others portrayed him as an enigma, a figure shrouded in mystery with an uncanny ability to vanish without a trace.

The lack of clarity and organisation in the files frustrated Elizabeth. She had hoped to find concrete evidence, a clear trail of David's activities that would lead her closer to understanding his true identity and intentions. Instead, she found herself sifting through a sea of conflicting accounts and unreliable information.

Undeterred by the confusion, Elizabeth knew that she had to approach the task with a methodical mindset. She began to compile a timeline of events, cross-referencing the reports to identify recurring themes or patterns. She meticulously analysed each piece of information, seeking connections and attempting to separate fact from speculation.

It became apparent to Elizabeth that David's methods were deliberately designed to obfuscate his true identity and intentions. His ability to blend in, manipulate information, and leave behind a trail of confusion had made him an elusive figure in the intelligence community.

And as she viewed these numerous files placed in front of her. She could help but see a sinister play in them. Not only was this confusing, but she suspected someone must have stirred up this confusion. She ran her hands through some files that were incomplete about David Scarlett. It would seem David has an insider who has deliberately removed some files and mixed up most of the information, so those who view it not only get awe-struck and invested, but they also get confused and frustrated because it was driving home no point. And the information were basically leading the readers in a circle.

Elizabeth sat on the desk, feeling a mix of frustration and concern as she dialled Joshua's number. She needed his perspective and advice on these missing files. Also, she wasn't sure she could keep the possibility of an insider within the S.I.S all to herself. After a few rings, Joshua picked up the call.

"Hey, Joshua," Elizabeth said, trying to keep her tone steady despite her growing unease.

"What's up, Liz," Joshua responded cheerfully.

"I've been going through the files on David Scarlett, and something doesn't add up. There are missing documents. It feels like there's someone within the S.I.S who's deliberately withholding information."

There was a brief pause on the other end of the line before Joshua responded. "Liz, I understand your concerns, but sometimes files go missing or get misplaced. It doesn't necessarily mean there's an insider involved. We shouldn't jump to conclusions just yet."

Elizabeth felt a pang of disappointment. She had hoped Joshua would share her suspicions and validate her concerns.

"I get what you're saying, Joshua," Elizabeth replied, trying not to sound paranoid "But these missing files seem too significant to be mere accidents. It's almost as if someone doesn't want us to have access to certain information about David Scarlett."

Joshua let out a sigh. "Look, I understand your point of view, Liz, but it's important not to let our imaginations run wild. We need concrete evidence before making any accusations. Have you considered seeking information from external sources?"

Elizabeth paused, considering Joshua's suggestion. He had always been logical and level-headed, providing a counterbalance to her sometimes impulsive tendencies.

"You might be onto something," Elizabeth admitted. "Perhaps it's time to approach this from a different angle. The rumours that David Scarlett had a background in law enforcement seem to be true. Maybe I should look into the police department in London where he was supposedly involved. They might have some records or insights that could shed light on his past."

"That sounds like a good plan," Joshua replied, his voice filled with encouragement. "The police department might have a different perspective on David's activities and could provide valuable information. Just be cautious, Liz. We don't know who we can trust at this point."

Elizabeth nodded, "I'll keep that in mind, Joshua. Thanks. I owe you one"

"Of course you do, Liz," Joshua responded warmly. "Stay safe out there."

Ending the call, Elizabeth couldn't help but feel a renewed sense of determination. She might not have received the validation she sought from Joshua, but at least she knows where to go next.

However, the thoughts of heading to the police department stare up a bit of anxiety in Elizabeth.
Her thoughts wandered back to the tragic event that had shaped her life—the murder of her father, who had served as an Officer of Duty in the police force in England.

The memory of that fateful day still lingered vividly in her mind. She had arrived home for her college break. She recalled the heart-wrenching phone call, the urgency in her mother's voice as she delivered the devastating news. Elizabeth had rushed to her father's office, only to find him lifeless in his chair, surrounded by the chaos of the crime scene. He had been shot in the chest three times.

The investigation that followed had been exhaustive, with countless leads pursued and suspects questioned. Yet, despite the best efforts of law enforcement, the perpetrator remained elusive, the truth shrouded in darkness. The pain of losing her father in such a senseless act of violence was a wound that refused to heal.

Elizabeth's determination to seek justice for her father had driven her decision to join the intelligence community. She believed fighting against corruption and criminal activities could honour her father's memory and bring some semblance of closure to his untimely death.

As she contemplated her next move in unravelling the mysteries surrounding David Scarlett, Elizabeth couldn't help but draw parallels between her father's case and the enigmatic figure she was pursuing. Both involved individuals who operated in the shadows, leaving a trail of unanswered questions and hidden truths.

But she realised she had found the strength to carry on with the sweet memories of him. That was all the strength she needed. Elizabeth refocused her attention on the task at hand. She knew that delving into the police records could potentially unearth connections and shed light on David Scarlett's activities during his time within the law enforcement community.

Waving off her anxiety, Elizabeth stood up and left the S.I.S facilities. She was going to the police department in London to request access to her father's case files and any relevant information that could lead her closer to the truth about David Scarlett and potentially bring her father's killer to justice.

As she walked the streets of London, memories of her father's warmth and dedication flooded her mind. She vowed to carry his legacy forward, fighting for justice and the protection of innocent lives from the darkness that lurked within the shadows.

Elizabeth took a deep breath as she entered the bustling police station. The sounds of ringing phones, hurried conversations, and shuffling paperwork filled the air, creating an atmosphere of controlled chaos. She glanced around, grateful that no one seemed to recognize her as the estranged daughter of Mason Morgan, the respected Officer of Duty whose murder had remained unsolved.

Keeping her identity concealed allowed Elizabeth to navigate the police station unnoticed, giving her the advantage of anonymity as she sought answers about David Scarlett. She knew that her family's history could potentially complicate matters and draw unnecessary attention. This investigation was about uncovering the truth, not personal connections or past grievances.

With her head held high and a determined expression on her face, Elizabeth approached the front desk, where a middle-aged officer was busy attending to a stack of paperwork.

"Excuse me," she said, her voice calm and confident. "I'm here to inquire about a former officer, David Scarlett. I believe he was involved in law enforcement in London. Is there anyone I could speak to regarding his records or any information you may have?"

The officer looked up, momentarily startled by Elizabeth's presence.

"David Scarlett, you say?" the officer replied, his tone cautious. "I'm afraid I can't disclose any information without proper authorization or a valid reason. Do you have any credentials or a specific purpose for your request?"

Elizabeth anticipated this response. She knew gaining access to sensitive information wouldn't be difficult, especially without a compelling reason or I.D. The S.I.S. had not permitted her to interact with the police department yet, and she was not about to wait through the whole bureaucracy progress to get that done. She knew she had to be persuasive without revealing her true motives to avoid getting in trouble.

"I understand the need for security and protocol," Elizabeth replied, maintaining her composed demeanour. "I'm conducting research on undercover operatives and their experiences within law enforcement agencies. I believe David Scarlett's background and activities could provide valuable insights into the field. My intention is to enhance our understanding of the challenges faced by those who dedicate their lives to maintaining law and order."

The officer's expression brightened, intrigued by Elizabeth's explanation.

He leaned forward, his curiosity piqued.

"I see," he responded, his tone less guarded. "That does sound like an interesting project. However, I'll need to consult with my superiors and verify your credentials before granting access to any sensitive information. If you could provide me with your contact information, we can follow up once we've received the necessary approvals."

Elizabeth nodded, appreciating the officer's willingness to consider her request. She jotted down her name, phone number, and a generic email address on a small notepad she carried with her.

"I understand," she replied, handing the notepad to the officer. "Here are my contact details. Please let your superiors know that I'm committed to maintaining the utmost confidentiality in handling any sensitive information."

The officer took the notepad, examining the details before offering a nod of acknowledgement.

"Thank you," he said, his tone more amicable. "I'll pass this along and get back to you as soon as I have an update. It may take a couple of days, considering the necessary clearance procedures."

That was not good. Going through the S.I.S bureaucracy was going to be faster than this. 'Is there no way we can speed things up? See, I'm kinda running out of time and...'

The officer gave Elizabeth a suspicious look. 'What are you getting at, ma'am?' he asked, staring her down. Elizabeth sighed and moved away from him. She looked around as she tried to figure out a way out.

A tall officer came out of a room down the hallway of the station and walked towards the middle-aged officer on the desk. 'Elizabeth Morgan?' he asked the young woman who backed him.

Elizabeth's heart skipped a beat as she turned to look and saw it was Officer Hugh Cross, the new Officer of Duty. She hadn't anticipated that her true identity would be discovered so quickly, especially by someone she was familiar with. Hugh's father had been her godfather, and they had shared many memories growing up. She couldn't help but cringe at the situation, unsure of how to proceed.

'What are you doing here?' he said as she turned around

"Hugh," she said, trying to regain her composure. "I didn't expect to run into you here. I'm... I'm..." she looked at the middle-aged officer 'well, I'm here for some research stuff.'

Hugh looked at her, a mix of surprise and concern evident in his eyes. He seemed taken aback by her presence.

"Why didn't you let me know you were coming?" he asked, his voice tinged with disappointment. "I could have helped you with your inquiries."

She sighed, realizing that her attempts to maintain anonymity had backfired.

It seemed that her presence at the police station had created a complicated situation, intertwining her personal and professional lives.

"I wanted to handle this on my own," Elizabeth replied, "I didn't want to burden you or anyone else with my own investigation. It's something I needed to do for myself."

Hugh studied her for a moment. 16 years of their childhood spent together, and Elizabeth had not changed. It was certainly Elizabeth he was looking at. The independent girl who believed she could do it all on her own. However, he also recognized she was there for something bigger than a research.

Elizabeth, on the other hand, couldn't take her eyes off ugh. Hugh Cross was a tall and imposing figure, standing head and shoulders above most people in the room. His well-built physique and muscular body structure spoke of a disciplined fitness routine and a commitment to physical strength. He carried himself with a sense of confidence and self-assurance that commanded attention.

His hair, a shade of blonde that caught the light and added a touch of warmth to his features, was styled in a regular cut that accentuated his handsome face. Though hints of balding were starting to appear, they did little to detract from his overall attractiveness. In fact, they seemed to add a touch of maturity and wisdom to his appearance, enhancing his rugged charm.

But it was his deep blue eyes that truly captivated those who met him. They sparkled with intelligence and a hint of mischief, drawing people in and making them feel seen and understood. It was in those eyes that Elizabeth had found solace and a sense of comfort during their childhood friendship. There was a familiarity and warmth in their gaze that had made her heart skip a beat more than once.

Hugh's smile was infectious, a charming grin that could light up a room and put people at ease. It revealed a row of perfectly aligned teeth, adding to his magnetic charm. His laughter was hearty and genuine, bringing joy to those around him. Elizabeth often found herself mesmerized by his smile, feeling a flutter of excitement whenever his lips curled into that familiar expression.

As childhood friends, Elizabeth and Hugh had shared many adventures and secrets. They had played together in the nearby park, exploring every nook and cranny, and creating memories that would last a lifetime. It was during those carefree days that Elizabeth's innocent crush had taken root, her admiration for Hugh growing stronger with each passing year.

Despite the passage of time and the challenges life had thrown their way, Hugh had remained a constant presence in Elizabeth's life. Their friendship had evolved and deepened over the years, becoming a bond built on trust, understanding, and shared experiences.

There was an unspoken connection between them, a familiarity and comfort that transcended words. They could communicate with a single glance, understand each other's thoughts without uttering a syllable.

It all came crashing down when Elizabeth's father got promoted, and they moved to a different neighbourhood separating Elizabeth and Hugh and breaching any form of friendship or connection they once had with kids.

Hugh's presence had a grounding effect on Elizabeth, providing her with a sense of security and reassurance. She knew that he would do whatever it took to protect her, to support her in her pursuit of justice for her father and in her quest to uncover the truth about David Scarlett. However, she was not sure she was comfortable having a childhood crush back in her life and space.

"Elizabeth, Your father was like a brother to my father, and we've known each other for years. Let me help you.' Hugh said. 'C'mon let's talk inside.' Elizabeth nodded and followed Hugh to his office.

,
When she got in and sat. She explained everything to Hugh. However, when Hugh replied, his revelation hit Elizabeth like a wave of confusion and disappointment. The rumour she had been chasing, the thread that could potentially lead her to David Scarlett, had turned out to be nothing more than hearsay.

"So, there's no record of David Scarlett ever working in the police department?" Elizabeth asked, her voice tinged with disbelief.

Hugh shook his head, his expression grave. "I've gone through our records for the past 20 years, and there's no trace of anyone by that name. The closest match is Officer Davidson Scarlett, who tragically lost his life a few years ago during a high-risk operation."

Elizabeth's disappointment deepened. She had hoped that her investigation would find a solid lead, a tangible connection to David Scarlett. But now, it seemed like she was back at square one, grappling with a name that held no weight or significance in the police department's records.

"Do you think there could be any connection between Officer Davidson

Scarlett and the David Scarlett I'm searching for?" Elizabeth inquired, her voice filled with uncertainty.

Hugh furrowed his brow, contemplating the possibility. "It's hard to say, Elizabeth. The names are similar, but without more information, it's purely speculation. I mean, apart from the fact that Officer Davidson was female and David Scarlett male. We can certainly dig deeper into Officer Davidson Scarlett's background and any potential connections she might have had to him. But, it's a long shot, and it's certainly a dead-end"

Elizabeth nodded absentmindedly, trying to process this information.

Hugh looked up, his eyes meeting Elizabeth's with a mix of concern and determination.

"Based on the information I've gathered over the years, it seems that David Scarlett had a penchant for assuming different identities," Hugh began. "He was skilled at blending in and disappearing into the shadows when necessary. It's possible that he used his abilities to conceal his true identity within the police force."

Elizabeth's curiosity was piqued. The revelation aligned with the disjointed and unclear files she had come across earlier. It seemed that David Scarlett was adept at operating undercover, going by different aliases and evading detection.

"He was a master of disguise, you mean?" she asked.

Hugh nodded, his gaze steady. "Yes, precisely. He had the ability to transform himself, adopting new identities that allowed him to move unnoticed in various circles. It's likely that he utilized these skills to navigate the world of espionage and covert operations."

Elizabeth contemplated the implications of this new information. David Scarlett's expertise in assuming different identities explained the confusion surrounding his records. It also made her task of uncovering the truth even more challenging.

"If he was so skilled at blending in, how do we even begin to find him?" Elizabeth wondered, a hint of frustration creeping into her voice.

Hugh leaned back in his chair, his expression thoughtful. "It won't be easy, Elizabeth. David Scarlett has undoubtedly left a trail of false identities and cover stories in his wake. But we can start by retracing his known activities and connections, examining any patterns or inconsistencies that might lead us to his current whereabouts. We'll need to dig deeper into his past, following any leads that might reveal his true identity."

Elizabeth nodded, recognizing the arduous task that lay ahead.

'Rumors swirled that Scarlett deliberately chose both male and female names to confuse those who sought to uncover his true gender and identity. Though, there have been numerous pieces of evidence that strongly suggest David Scarlett is a man," Hugh explained, his voice carrying a sense of conviction. "While he may have initially used different names to sow confusion and create a veil of uncertainty, our investigations have pointed towards his true gender."

Elizabeth's brow furrowed as she absorbed this information. The complexity of Scarlett's methods and the lengths he had gone to conceal his true identity were becoming increasingly apparent. She realized that she would have to navigate a web of misdirection and deliberate obfuscation in her pursuit of the truth.

"What kind of evidence do we have that indicates he is a man?" she asked, her voice laced with curiosity.

Hugh reached for a folder on his desk and retrieved several photographs. He handed them to Elizabeth, who eagerly examined the images. The photographs depicted a shadowy and foggy all-male suspect embodied in various locations, undertaking covert operations and interacting with other individuals.

"These photographs were captured during surveillance operations," Hugh explained. "They were obtained from reliable sources within our intelligence networks. As you can see, they clearly show that David Scarlett has embodied in all these numerous operations. They all have masculine features, including his facial structure, body language, and physical build."

Elizabeth scrutinized the photographs, studying Scarlett's features closely. It was evident that the person in the images possessed distinct masculine attributes.

"Although he may have deliberately chosen ambiguous allies to confuse his pursuers, his true gender has become more apparent as we gather more evidence," Hugh continued. "It seems that his strategy was to maintain a level of uncertainty and keep his adversaries guessing, which allowed him to operate more effectively within his espionage network."

"I can't afford to make assumptions or underestimate his methods," Elizabeth said with her voice filled with determination. "I have to be thorough in our investigation and consider all possibilities. Scarlett's ability to deceive is a testament to his skill and cunning."

Hugh nodded in agreement. 'The extent of his network and the true purpose behind his elusive nature remained a mystery, but there was no denying the significant impact he had made through numerous high-profile heists across the globe. Governments and intelligence agencies worldwide had taken notice and were calling for Scarlett to be stopped.'

Elizabeth's eyebrow furrowed. 'Is this serious?'

"David Scarlett's actions have caused significant concern and disruption on an international scale," Hugh explained, his voice tinged with a mix of urgency and concern. "He has orchestrated daring heists that have targeted valuable assets, sensitive information, and even top-secret government facilities. The ramifications of his activities extend far beyond individual incidents."

Elizabeth's eyes widened as she grasped the gravity of the situation. No wonder everyone in the S.I.S. was fidgeting. The fact that he had managed to evade capture and maintain his clandestine operations for an extended period indicated a level of sophistication and cunning that no one could ignore anymore'.

"Scarlett's actions have raised serious concerns among government officials and intelligence agencies worldwide. His operations have the potential implications of compromising national security and destabilizing international relations. It cannot be ignored anymore."

"So it is not just about apprehending him as an individual; it is about safeguarding the interests of nations and protecting innocent lives.' The realization that Scarlett's actions were not merely for personal gain but had wider implications for global stability and security added an additional layer to the sense of urgency of this mission.

Hugh nodded, "You are right, Elizabeth.' Hugh paused for a moment and continued.

'Take this with a pinch of salt. It's just my little personal opinion on Scarlett. I think at this point I could be considered a Scarlett fanboy with my trailing of him over the years,' Hugh smiled, and Elizabeth chuckled 'But I don't believe David Scarlett is just an individual. I think it's more of an organized crime organization than an individual.'

"An organized crime organization?" Elizabeth echoed, her voice filled with curiosity and intrigue. "That would explain the level of sophistication and the seamless coordination in Scarlett's operations.' Elizabeth's eyes widened in surprise at Hugh's revelation. 'But, who is behind this organization? And how do we find them?"

Hugh leaned back in his chair, contemplating the question. "Unfortunately, we don't have all the answers yet," he admitted.

Elizabeth nodded, her mind already racing with possibilities. "If we can identify the key players, we might be able to find the cracks in their system. I mean, every organization, no matter how well-structured, has vulnerabilities. We just need to find them and exploit them to our advantage."

"Exactly. We'll need to delve deeper into Scarlett's past operations, analyze his targets, and look for any recurring patterns. We should also explore any possible connections he might have, whether it's financial, technological, or even personal relationships. There might be individuals or entities linked to him that can provide valuable leads."

Elizabeth furrowed her brow, thinking out loud. "We also need to consider his motivations. What drives this organization? Is it purely financial gain, or is there a larger agenda at play? Understanding their motives might help us anticipate their next moves and uncover their hidden agenda."

"Absolutely.' Hugh paused and excused himself. He came back with a file and handed it to Elizabeth.

Elizabeth accepted the file from Hugh, her eyes fixed on its contents. As she opened the file, she discovered a series of surveillance photos, documents, and background information on the man they had been trailing.

"This is interesting," Elizabeth remarked, studying the photos closely. "Who is this?"

Hugh leaned forward, pointing to a particular photo. "His name is Thomas Crane," he said. "We believe he has close ties to David Scarlett, although we haven't been able to gather enough evidence to make an arrest yet. Crane is a skilled operative and has managed to stay one step ahead of us."

Elizabeth's mind raced as she absorbed the details in the file. "What do we know about his role within the organization?'

Hugh leaned back in his chair. "Crane is a highly elusive figure, much like Scarlett himself. He operates in the shadows, carrying out covert operations for the organization. Our intelligence suggests that he is involved in a wide range of activities, from espionage and hacking to financial manipulation. He's a key player in the organization, but we're still working on piecing together his exact role and responsibilities."

Elizabeth nodded, her determination growing stronger. "If we can gather more information on Crane's activities, we might be able to establish a stronger link to David Scarlett.'

"Absolutely.' Hugh agreed, his eyes gleaming with a mix of caution and excitement. 'But you need to be careful, Liz. These are confidential files, and their operations mustn't be opened to the public. Be careful around Crane.'

'You know you can count on me, Hugh' Elizabeth smiled

Hugh's smile widened as he watched Elizabeth smile. It was good to have her smile this good.

"It's good to have you back in London," Hugh said warmly. It had been more than a decade of them being apart, but he still could help but feel the same way he felt those years.

As Elizabeth caught the glint in Hugh's eyes, she couldn't help but feel a flicker of uncertainty and curiosity. The memories of their childhood friendship flashed through her mind, reminding her of the innocent connection they once shared.

She couldn't deny that there had always been a certain chemistry between them, even during their younger years. Hugh's charm and charisma had made him a popular figure, catching the attention of many. Elizabeth had seen his playboy nature firsthand, and she had made a conscious decision to guard her heart against any potential hurt.

Now, standing before him as adults, those unresolved feelings and unanswered questions resurfaced, stirring a mixture of emotions within Elizabeth. She found herself torn between the past and the present, unsure of what she truly felt for Hugh and uncertain about his intentions.

"It's good to see you, Hugh.' Elizabeth said. Everything they had and shared spiralled down when her dad got a promotion, and they had to move to a different neighbourhood. Hugh and Elizabeth never got to see each other again and moved on with their teenage lives.

Hugh's gaze held hers for a moment longer before he sighed softly, his expression transitioning from a glimmer of something more to a composed professionalism. 'You have a long case ahead of you.' he said and winked.

Elizabeth nodded, and smiled. Hugh was still the same man. Serious minded and dedicated to whatsoever he gets himself into. It was good to see her friend was still the same person he was about a decade ago. Yet, he could see into her heart and tell how she felt towards him. Perhaps, there could be something more.

Suppressing her own feelings, Elizabeth pushed those thoughts aside and regained her composure. "Certainly, Hugh.'

She got up and headed for the door while Hugh stood up to join her and show her the way out.

As she walked the streets, a small part of her couldn't help but hope this feeling could grow to be something bigger and richer for both of them.

CHAPTER THREE: UNCOVERING CLUES

As Elizabeth stepped into Crane's flower shop, she found herself enveloped in a symphony of colours, fragrances, and natural beauty. The shop was a sanctuary of floral delights, a place where nature's gifts were carefully curated and displayed. It was a haven that ignited the senses and invited a moment of tranquillity in the bustling city.

The entrance of the shop beckoned with a charming wooden door adorned with a delicate wreath of freshly cut flowers. As she pushed the door open, a gentle chime tinkled, announcing her arrival. The interior was a harmonious blend of rustic charm and contemporary elegance, creating an atmosphere that was both inviting and sophisticated.

Sunlight streamed through large windows, casting a soft glow on the meticulously arranged bouquets and potted plants that adorned every corner of the shop. The shelves were lined with a myriad of vases in various shapes and sizes, each holding its own unique arrangement. From vibrant roses to delicate orchids, from cheerful daisies to exotic lilies, the floral displays showcased the richness and diversity of nature's palette.

The air was infused with the intoxicating scents of blossoms, creating an olfactory symphony that danced around Elizabeth. With every breath, she could detect the sweet fragrance of roses, the earthy aroma of freshly cut stems, and the subtle hints of jasmine and lavender. It was as if the very essence of nature had been captured within the confines of this enchanting space.

The shop itself was adorned with whimsical touches, adding a touch of whimsy and elegance to the surroundings. Delicate fairy lights twinkled overhead, casting a soft, ethereal glow. A vintage chandelier hung gracefully from the ceiling, its crystals catching the light and casting shimmering patterns on the walls. And in the corners, charming antique furniture displayed delicate vases, framed photographs, and books on the art of floral arrangements, offering a glimpse into the world of flowers.

Elizabeth walked along the aisles, taking in the meticulous displays that showcased the beauty of each bloom. She marvelled at the artistry and skill that went into the arrangements, the way colours and textures were harmoniously combined to create masterpieces that seemed to breathe with life.

The shop was not only a place to purchase flowers; it was a sanctuary for the senses, a respite from the chaos of the outside world. Soft instrumental music played in the background, providing a soothing melody that further enhanced the serene ambience. Customers, dressed in an array of styles, meandered through the shop, their faces adorned with awe and delight as they discovered the perfect bouquet for their loved ones or themselves.

Elizabeth discreetly observed Mr Lawrence from a corner of his flower shop, her eyes fixed on the unassuming middle-aged man with glasses. She had expected someone different, perhaps a young and eerie-looking individual with a scar on his face, as the rumours surrounding David Scarlett had led her to believe. However, what she saw before her was a quiet figure, blending seamlessly into the environment.

Mr Lawrence, as the other shopkeepers called him, appeared to be in his mid-40s, with salt-and-pepper hair neatly combed back. His gentle demeanour and unassuming presence made it difficult to imagine him as someone connected to the elusive David Scarlett. He seemed engrossed in attending to the needs of the customers, offering advice and suggestions on the perfect flowers for their occasions.

Elizabeth noticed the finesse with which Mr Lawrence handled each interaction. His attentive eyes sparkled with genuine interest as he listened to customers' preferences, guiding them with a wealth of knowledge about the different varieties, their meanings, and the best ways to care for them. His soft-spoken nature and warm smile seemed to put everyone at ease.

It was intriguing to Elizabeth how Mr Lawrence seamlessly integrated into the routine of the flower shop. He worked diligently, arranging bouquets with precision and artistry, displaying an intimate understanding of the delicate balance between colours, textures, and shapes. His hands moved with grace and purpose, creating arrangements that were both visually stunning and emotionally evocative.

As Elizabeth watched, she couldn't help but notice the trust and familiarity that the other shopkeepers showed towards Mr Lawrence. They exchanged friendly banter and occasionally sought his opinion on matters unrelated to flowers. It was evident that he had become an integral part of their small community, respected not only for his expertise in the floral arts but also for his kind and reliable nature.

While Elizabeth couldn't deny her curiosity about Mr. Lawrence's possible connection to David Scarlett, she knew better than to jump to conclusions. She reminded herself that appearances could be deceiving, and that the truth often hid behind the most unexpected facades.

Mr. Lawrence, the unassuming figure in the flower shop, appeared to be an ordinary middle-aged man at first glance, but as Elizabeth observed him closely, she sensed that there was more to him than met the eye.

His most striking feature was his bright blue eyes, which seemed to hold a depth and intensity that contradicted his calm and composed demeanour. They were the kind of eyes that revealed the weight of life's experiences, the stories and secrets hidden behind their gaze. Elizabeth couldn't help but be drawn to those eyes, captivated by the enigma they portrayed.

As she observed Mr. Lawrence, she noticed the lines etched on his face, subtle creases that spoke of a life lived with both triumphs and challenges. These were the remnants of his youth, a reminder of a time when his face held promises that had faded away with the passing years. Yet, beneath the facade of maturity and experience, Elizabeth sensed something more, something menacing lurking within.

It was in the subtle shifts of his expressions, the way his eyes flickered momentarily with an intensity that sent shivers down her spine. It was as if a dark shadow concealed behind the mask of geniality occasionally revealed itself, hinting at a hidden darkness. Elizabeth couldn't quite put her finger on it, but there was an aura of danger surrounding Mr. Lawrence, an unspoken presence that seemed to echo through his very being.

Despite the disquieting feeling he evoked, Mr. Lawrence carried himself with grace and poise, moving with a calculated precision as he attended to the needs of the customers. His movements were deliberate, his hands deftly arranging flowers with expertise that belied his unassuming appearance. There was a certain artistry to his actions, as if he possessed a deep understanding of the language spoken by petals and stems.

As Elizabeth discreetly observed him, she noticed how effortlessly he interacted with the customers, offering gentle smiles and advice with a professionalism that bespoke years of experience. His voice, though calm and measured, carried a hint of authority, a subtle command that demanded attention. It was as if he knew the power he held, the knowledge that lay within him, and revealed in the control it afforded him.

It was this sense of control that further fueled Elizabeth's unease. Beneath the facade of a humble florist, she knew that he was more than what he had made himself to be. His ability to seamlessly blend into the shop's routine, his connection with the other shopkeepers, and the respect he commanded all hinted at a deeper involvement, a web of influence that extended beyond the walls of the flower shop.

But what troubled Elizabeth the most was the feeling of being studied whenever Mr Lawrence's gaze briefly met hers. It was as if he saw through her, penetrating the layers of her own facade, and glimpsing the determination and purpose that fueled her investigation. The glint in his bright blue eyes held a knowingness that sent a chill down her spine, an unspoken warning that she was treading in dangerous waters.

As Elizabeth reluctantly tore her gaze away from Mr Lawrence, she couldn't shake the lingering feeling of trepidation that clung to her. The menacing undercurrent she sensed beneath his calm exterior only fueled her resolve to approach him

Elizabeth turned and cautiously approached Mr. Lawrence, she couldn't help but notice a subtle shift in his demeanour. The warm smile that had graced his face moments ago seemed to fade, replaced by a cool detachment. It was as if he had anticipated her approach, as if he knew who she was without uttering a single word.

His bright blue eyes, once captivating and full of depth, now seemed to hold a hint of suspicion and wariness. They bore into her own gaze, piercing through the layers of her own facade and leaving her feeling exposed and vulnerable. Elizabeth couldn't shake the feeling that Mr. Lawrence possessed a knowledge beyond what she could comprehend. As if he had seen through her carefully constructed cover and unravelled the secrets she held within.

There was a silence that hung heavy in the air as Elizabeth stood before him. The tension between them was palpable, a silent dance of unspoken words and hidden intentions. She could sense that Mr. Lawrence was guarded, his walls firmly in place, shielding whatever truths lay behind his enigmatic persona.

As she searched for words, Elizabeth found herself caught between curiosity and caution. She was aware that any misstep could have dire consequences, she was not meant to be there in the first place. Yet, her determination to uncover the truth pushed her forward, refusing to let fear dictate her actions.

"Mr. Lawrence, I have been led to believe that you may have some knowledge regarding a man named David Scarlett. I seek the truth and hope that you might be willing to shed some light on the matter." Elizabeth finally spoke, her voice steady, almost too steady as she tried to suppress any tinge with a hint of apprehension.

There was a flicker of emotion in Mr. Lawrence's eyes, a fleeting glimpse of something that Elizabeth couldn't quite decipher. It was a mixture of wariness, curiosity, and perhaps a hint of resignation. 'I've never had a customer with such a name.' he finally said with an air of indifference.

Elizabeth smiled and cleared her throat. He was certainly not ready to open up. But she was more than ready to open him up 'maybe you didn't hear me correctly. I'm going to ask that question once again, Mr. Lawrence...or should I say Mr. Crane?

The mention of his real name seemed to strike a nerve, causing a flicker of unease to pass across his features. His eyes darted around the room, as if searching for an escape, before settling back on her with a guarded intensity.

"What do you mean by Crane?" he muttered, his voice tinged with a mix of surprise and caution. "No one bares that name. It is best you leave now and forget what you have seen." Crane moved to show Elizabeth the way out.

Determined not to be deterred, Elizabeth pressed on, her voice steady but tinged with urgency. "I believe there is a connection between you and David Scarlett. Why are you afraid of letting these lovely people know who you are?'

Mr. Lawrence's eyes bore into her own, as if he was searching for something she couldn't quite discern. His jaw tightened, and his body seemed to stiffen with a mix of apprehension and defiance. After a brief silence that hung heavily in the air.

"You are treading dangerous ground," he warned, his voice laced with a sense of resignation. "Crane was a name I left behind, a past I buried deep within the recesses of my being. It is a name best forgotten, for both your sake and mine."

Elizabeth's heart quickened with a mixture of anticipation and apprehension. She knew this was it, that Crane held vital information, information that could unveil the enigma of David Scarlett. Yet, his reluctance to reveal his true identity and connection to Crane only deepened her resolution to get the truth out of him.

"I understand that you wish to protect yourself," Elizabeth spoke softly, her eyes never leaving his. "But if there is a chance to bring justice and peace to those affected by David Scarlett's actions, I implore you to reconsider. Help me uncover the truth. What do you know about him?'

Crane gave out a loud and deep sound laughter that had a crackle to it. The laughter was so loud it got the attention of everyone in the shop for a moment. This made Elizabeth feel even more unease than her first encounter with him.

Crane's demeanor soon shifted once again to a menacing look, almost like he had switched personality in a blink of an eye. The tension that had filled the room heightened, he move closer to Elizabeth.

"I am Crane," he confessed, his voice firm and threatening. "And my connection to David Scarlett is none of your business. Now get out!'

As Elizabeth walked away from Mr. Lawrence's flower shop, a sense of frustration and curiosity gnawed at her. In the hopes to glean some information about David Scarlett, the encounter had left her with more questions than answers.

Her mind raced with possibilities, trying to piece together the fragments of what she had observed and the tidbits of information she had gathered so far. She couldn't shake the feeling that Mr. Lawrence held key insights into the truth she sought, but his guarded nature had thwarted her attempts to uncover them.

As she wandered through the bustling streets of London, Elizabeth's determination only grew stronger. She knew that she couldn't rely solely on one lead or one encounter to uncover the depths of David Scarlett's web of intrigue. She would need to cast her net wider, dig deeper, and follow every thread that hinted at his existence.

Still, Crane was the only clue to David Scarlett that she was aware of. Elizabeth's mind raced as she tried to come up with a plan to get Crane to open up about David Scarlett.

As she walked through the bustling streets of London, Elizabeth contemplated different approaches. The direct approach has definitely failed with Crane, as he had already shown resistance to revealing anything. She needed a more subtle and strategic approach.

One idea crossed her mind. She decided to dig deeper into Crane's background and gather more information about him. Perhaps there were clues hidden within his personal life or connections that could shed light on his association with David Scarlett.

She got her phone from her pocket to call someone in the office. As she was about to dial, she felt some shadowy figures passed her. Elizabeth lifted up her eyes and saw four men in black match towards Crane's shop. She turned away, ignoring the scenery. But she could help but look back.

The men in black had entered Crane's shop. Though she initially brushed it off, a nagging sense of unease began to settle within her. She couldn't shake the feeling that something was amiss.

Suddenly, Elizabeth's heart skipped a beat as she heard the sound of gunshots coming from inside Crane's shop. Without hesitation, she instinctively rushed towards the source of the commotion, driven by a mix of concern for Crane and her own determination to uncover the truth.

As she entered the shop, a scene of chaos unfolded before her. The once serene flower shop was now filled with shattered glass, overturned shelves, and panicked customers. Elizabeth's eyes scanned the room, desperately searching for any sign of Crane amidst the mayhem.

Amidst the chaos, she spotted a figure lying motionless on the floor. Fear gripped her heart as she realized it was Crane. She hurriedly made her way towards him, navigating through the debris with a sense of urgency.

As she knelt beside Crane, her heart sank. It was clear that he had been seriously injured. Blood stained his clothes, and his breathing was shallow. Elizabeth's mind raced, assessing the situation. She reached for her phone and dialled for emergency services.

As Elizabeth waited for the paramedics to arrive, she cradled Crane's head in her lap. Her heart sank as she saw the extent of his injuries. Blood stained his face, and he was struggling to stay conscious. She knew she had to act quickly if she wanted to get any information on David Scarlett.

With urgency in her voice, Elizabeth pleaded, "Crane, you have to stay with me. I need answers. Tell me about David Scarlett, about your connection to him."

Crane's eyes fluttered, and he weakly whispered, "You... don't understand."

Elizabeth pressed on, trying to keep him alert. "I need to know, Crane. Who did this to you?"

As Crane struggled to use his last remaining breath, his voice barely a whisper, he managed to utter one final phrase: "Foul play... foul..." His words hung in the air, filled with a sense of urgency and warning, leaving Elizabeth with more questions than answers.

The weight of those words resonated within her, igniting a fire of determination to uncover the truth behind the enigma of David Scarlett and the darkness that surrounded him. Crane's utterance suggested that there was more to the story, that hidden forces were at play, manipulating events behind the scenes.

Elizabeth's mind raced, contemplating the implications of Crane's words. What did he mean by "foul play"? Was he referring to the attack on him or something more insidious? It was clear that there were hidden motives and sinister forces at work, weaving a web of deception that threatened to engulf them all.

As Elizabeth cradled Crane in her lap, she couldn't help but notice the look of horror etched upon his face. His blood-stained features seemed to contort with anguish, his eyes wide with fear and disbelief. It was a haunting expression that sent shivers down Elizabeth's spine.

Crane's lips quivered as he struggled to speak, his voice strained and barely audible. The pain in his eyes was palpable, as if he had witnessed unimaginable horrors and carried the weight of his knowledge with a heavy burden.

The lines of his face were etched with despair, his brow furrowed with deep worry. Sweat mingled with the blood on his forehead, highlighting the intensity of his suffering. His once lively eyes, now clouded with pain, conveyed a profound sense of helplessness.

Elizabeth could see that Crane was on the precipice of something unspeakable, caught between the harrowing secrets he carried and the overwhelming danger that lurked in the shadows. It was as if the horrors he had witnessed had imprinted themselves on his very being, leaving an indelible mark.

Crane's gasps for breath were mixed with coughs, and blood trickled from his mouth, staining his teeth and lips. His body trembled with the strain, his muscles tense as he fought against the encroaching darkness. Yet, through it all, a glimmer of determination flickered in his eyes, as if he was desperately clinging to a sliver of hope.

In that moment, Elizabeth couldn't help but feel a profound sense of empathy and sorrow for the man before her. The look of horror on Crane's face mirrored the weight of the knowledge he possessed, the horrors he had encountered, and the imminent threat that overshadowed his existence. It was a visceral reflection of the treacherous path he had walked, a glimpse into the abyss of darkness that consumed his world.

Crane's consciousness slipped away, and his face frozen in a mask of terror. Elizabeth gently closed his eyes. She got up and looked around. The paramedics had not arrived yet. And so that moment, an idea popped into her mind. Maybe Crane had something in the shop that could bring her a step closer to David Scarlett. So she got up and walked across the shop searching for anything she could find on David Scarlett.

As Elizabeth frantically searched through Crane's shop, her heart pounding with a mixture of anticipation and anxiety, she meticulously combed through every file, unlocking every box, and inspecting every nook and cranny, desperately seeking answers.

The air in the shop felt heavy, charged with tension and a sense of urgency. The faint scent of flowers still lingered, intermingling with the scent of blood, creating a surreal atmosphere. The shelves lined with bouquets and arrangements seemed to silently witness the turmoil unfolding within the small space.

Elizabeth's hands trembled as she sifted through papers, photographs, and various objects, her eyes scanning each item in the hope of finding a hidden compartment or a secret passage that might reveal the truth. The sound of her own breath seemed amplified, echoing through the silent shop, as she delved deeper into the mysteries hidden within its walls.

But despite her thorough search, Elizabeth found no concrete evidence or definitive answers. The absence of any conclusive findings only deepened the mystery surrounding Crane, David Scarlett, and the forces that were at play. It was as if the truth had been expertly concealed, leaving behind nothing but a trail of questions and speculation. Perhaps the men in black took it with them.

Frustration welled up within her, mixed with a tinge of disappointment. She had hoped that Crane's shop would hold the key to unlocking the secrets that had eluded her so far. Yet, the barrenness of the search left her with an unsettling realization: the answers she sought were not to be found in this physical realm alone.

In the face of this setback, Elizabeth resolved to widen her perspective, to delve into the realms beyond the tangible. She knew that the truth often lay hidden in the intangible, in the connections between seemingly unrelated events, in the whispers of shadows and the echoes of secrets.

As she stepped out onto the bustling streets of London, Elizabeth carried with her the weight of unanswered questions, and the echoes of Crane's final words. She would not rest until she unraveled the intricate web of deceit and exposed the truth that lay shrouded in darkness.

CHAPTER FOUR: A TRAIL OF SHADOWS

As Elizabeth woke up, her mind instantly raced to the events of the previous day. The urgency of her mission and the consequences of her actions weighed heavily on her thoughts. She knew that her unauthorized involvement in Crane's shop and the local London police investigation had caught the attention of the S.I.S, and now she was summoned for a disciplinary check.

Elizabeth's mind was consumed by the weight of her actions and the potential repercussions that awaited her. She knew that her impulsive behaviour had jeopardized the trust and confidentiality she shared with Hugh. As she thought about the consequences of her actions, a deep sense of remorse washed over her.

She understood that Hugh had provided her with valuable information in confidence, trusting that she would handle it responsibly. Yet, she had allowed her desperation to cloud her judgment, leading her to cross boundaries and violate that trust. The murder at Crane's shop was a stark reminder of the dangers lurking in her investigation and the collateral damage caused by her recklessness.

Now, Elizabeth grappled with the consequences of her actions and the inevitable confrontation with Hugh. She respected him not only as a childhood friend and confidant but also as a skilled officer of the law. His disappointment and anger were justifiable, and she couldn't bear the thought of losing his support and friendship.

As she contemplated her next steps, Elizabeth realized that she needed to make amends and rebuild the trust she had broken. She would approach Hugh with honesty and humility, acknowledging her mistakes and taking responsibility for her actions. It would be a difficult conversation, but she knew it was necessary to salvage their relationship and secure his continued cooperation.

In the meantime, Elizabeth resolved to exercise caution and restraint in her investigation. She would adhere to the proper channels, respecting the boundaries set by the S.I.S. and local law enforcement.

However, while lying in bed, she contemplated her next move, knowing that her every decision could shape the course of her investigation and potentially lead her closer or away from David Scarlett. The options stretched out before her like a vast landscape, each one carrying its own risks and rewards.

She considered the possibility of cooperating with the S.I.S., sharing the limited information she had gathered so far and seeking their assistance in her pursuit of the truth. However, she hesitated, mindful of the potential repercussions and the risk of losing control over her investigation. She knew that certain factions within the intelligence community might have their own agendas and could hinder her progress.

Another option that crossed her mind was to go rogue, operating independently and staying off the radar of official channels. This would allow her the freedom to delve deeper into the mystery surrounding David Scarlett without being bound by bureaucracy or compromised by external influences. Yet, she understood the inherent dangers of such an approach, as it would put her at odds with the very organizations she sought to bring down.

Taking a deep breath, Elizabeth made a decision. She would tread a fine line, maintaining a delicate balance between cooperation and autonomy. She would cautiously navigate the intricate web of intelligence agencies, leveraging their resources and expertise while safeguarding the integrity of her investigation.

With a clear plan in mind, Elizabeth rose from bed, her resolve solidified. She would attend the disciplinary check with the S.I.S, answering their questions honestly but withholding the finer details of her pursuit. She would choose her words carefully, not revealing her true intentions or the extent of her knowledge.

After the meeting, she would continue her relentless pursuit of the truth, gathering more information, connecting the dots, and following the faint trails that might lead her closer to David Scarlett. She knew it would be a perilous journey, fraught with danger and uncertainty, but she was prepared to face the challenges head-on.

As she got ready for the day ahead, Elizabeth embraced the gravity of her mission. She understood that the road ahead would test her in ways she couldn't yet comprehend, but she was determined to honour her father's memory and fulfil her own destiny.

Elizabeth stepped outside and waited for a taxi to arrive. In a minute, she wave down a Taxi and entered. Inside the taxi, Elizabeth settled into the comfortable upholstery, feeling the familiar hum of the engine beneath her. She gave the driver the address of her next destination, leaning back in the comfortable leather seats of the taxi as it smoothly made its way through the bustling streets of London. The soft jazz music playing on the radio provided a soothing backdrop to her thoughts.

As the taxi made its way through the city streets, Elizabeth gazed out of the window, watching the vibrant city life unfold. People hurriedly crossed the streets, umbrellas bobbed in the rain, and the cityscape stretched out before her in a mix of old and new architecture. London's charm and energy were palpable, even from within the confines of the taxi.

Lost in her thoughts, Elizabeth appreciated the brief respite the taxi ride offered. It was a moment of solitude amidst the fast-paced world she inhabited. The gentle swaying of the vehicle and the rhythmic sound of the rain on the roof provided a soothing backdrop, allowing her to gather her thoughts and prepare for the next chapter of her mission.

She took a moment to collect her thoughts and prepare for her visit to the S.I.S office. The interior of the cab provided a temporary refuge, shielding her from the bustling streets of London. However, her moment of respite was abruptly shattered when the taxi driver turned to face her.

The man's piercing gaze locked onto Elizabeth, his eyes filled with an intensity that sent a shiver down her spine. His voice carried a cold and menacing tone as he addressed her by her full name, "Agent Elizabeth Morgan." The shock and unease washed over her, leaving her feeling vulnerable and on edge.

Her mind raced, desperately trying to recall any previous encounters or connections with this mysterious figure. Yet, she drew a blank, realizing that she had never met this man before. Questions flooded her mind. How did he know her name? What was his purpose in addressing her in such a direct and unsettling manner?

"How do you know my name?" Elizabeth asked, her voice filled with a mix of curiosity and apprehension. The taxi driver remained silent for a moment, his gaze fixed on her as if weighing his next words. Finally, he spoke, his voice low and filled with a sense of urgency.

"I have my sources," he replied cryptically, his tone conveying a subtle warning. "Just watch your back, Agent Elizabeth Morgan."

Elizabeth's instincts kicked in, urging her to remain cautious and vigilant. She observed the man's demeanour, noting the subtle signs of threat and danger that seemed to emanate from him. The atmosphere in the taxi suddenly became suffocating.

'Did David Scarlett send you to me?' Elizabeth asked, suppressing her rising anxiety,

But they had already arrived at the S.I.S headquarters. Elizabeth quickly got out while the mysterious taxi driver zoomed off quickly

She desperately wanted to pursue him, to demand answers, but he was far beyond her reach. Elizabeth straightened up and walked into the headquarters.

As Elizabeth made her way into the S.I.S. office, her thoughts were in turmoil. The encounter with the mysterious taxi driver had ignited a new sense of urgency within her. She knew that she had to be cautious, to watch her back as he had warned.

Elizabeth composed herself as she walked through the office corridors. She was determined to face the panel with honesty and integrity, to explain her actions and prove her commitment to the S.I.S and its mission.

Elizabeth took a deep breath as she entered the disciplinary panel room. The atmosphere was tense, and the stern expressions on the faces of the panel members only added to her apprehension. The room was filled with an air of authority and expectation, with each panel member exuding a commanding presence.

The panel consisted of a diverse group of senior officials, both men and women, who had years of experience in the intelligence community. They were known for their astute judgment and strict adherence to protocol. As Elizabeth stood before them, she couldn't help but feel the weight of their collective scrutiny.

Their frowns were etched with a sternness that seemed to penetrate her very core. Elizabeth understood that she was about to face a gruelling interrogation, where every word and action would be scrutinized. The room seemed to grow colder, and the silence amplified her nerves.

She reminded herself to remain composed and focused, relying on her training and inner strength. The panel members may have appeared intimidating, but Elizabeth knew that she had to present her case with confidence and conviction.

Taking her place at the centre of the room, Elizabeth met the panel's gaze head-on. She maintained eye contact, conveying her determination and readiness to address their concerns. As the questioning began, she listened attentively, carefully considering each question before providing her response.

The disciplinary panel room was a grand hall, designed to convey a sense of authority and seriousness. The space was expansive, with high ceilings that seemed to stretch into infinity. The room was bathed in a soft, muted light, giving it an almost ethereal ambience.

At the centre of the room stood a roundtable, reserved exclusively for the panel members. It was an imposing structure, crafted from a combination of steel and silver, with a polished surface that gleamed under the subdued lighting. The table was large enough to comfortably accommodate the panel members, their documents, and any additional materials they might need during the proceedings.

Surrounding the roundtable were eight giant chairs, each meticulously placed equidistant from one another. These chairs were elevated, signifying the elevated status of the panel members who would be presiding over the proceedings. The chairs were upholstered in rich, dark leather, exuding an air of authority and sophistication.

The walls of the room were adorned with minimalistic artwork, consisting of abstract pieces that reflected the austere nature of the space. The artwork featured monochromatic tones, predominantly black and white, adding to the overall atmosphere of seriousness and formality. The steel and silver accents continued along the walls, creating a seamless flow between the architectural elements and the interior design.

The floor of the room was a polished marble, its surface reflecting the subtle light and adding to the room's pristine appearance. The marble had a cool, smooth texture underfoot, reinforcing the overall sense of sharpness and precision in the room.

The room was meticulously organized, with a designated space for each panel member. Each chair was positioned in alignment with the roundtable, ensuring that every panel member had an unobstructed view of Elizabeth as she stood before them. The placement of the chairs also facilitated efficient communication and collaboration among the panel members during the proceedings.

Despite its grandeur, the room exuded a certain coldness and stiffness. The steel and silver elements, combined with the minimalistic design, created an atmosphere that was both imposing and rigid. The room seemed to demand respect and compliance, reminding all who entered of the gravity of the situation at hand.

As Elizabeth stood in the centre of the room, she felt the weight of the space bearing down on her. The sharp edges and pristine surfaces were weight in the seriousness of the proceedings. She understood that within this room, decisions would be made that could shape the course of her career and future.

Elizabeth's gaze fell upon a woman standing in front of the community. The woman, like Elizabeth, exudes a certain air of confidence and poise. She had a striking appearance that commanded attention.

Her short blonde haircut framed her face elegantly, accentuating her sharp features. The carefully styled locks fell just above her shoulders, adding a touch of sophistication to her overall look. Her hair appeared to have a subtle shine, catching the light in the room and creating a luminous effect.

The young woman's eyes were mesmerizing. They were a piercing shade of blue, reminiscent of the vast ocean on a clear day. Her gaze seemed to penetrate through anyone who dared to meet her eyes, leaving an indelible impression. There was a mysterious depth to her gaze, hinting at a wealth of knowledge and experience beyond her years.

Her facial features were well-defined and symmetrical. A slender, straight nose led the way to her soft, perfectly shaped lips. Her lips were adorned with a dark crimson lipstick, adding a touch of allure and sensuality to her otherwise composed demeanour. The colour contrasted beautifully against her fair complexion, leaving a lasting impression.

The young woman's attire exuded a sense of professionalism and sophistication. She wore a tailored suit, much like Elizabeth, but with a unique twist. The suit was impeccably fitted, accentuating her slender figure. The jacket hugged her form, emphasizing her strong and confident presence. The trousers flowed gracefully, elongating her legs and adding to her overall stature.

Her choice of colour for the suit was a deep navy blue, exuding elegance and authority. The fabric appeared to be of high quality, with a subtle sheen that caught the light and added a touch of glamour. The suit was impeccably tailored, with clean lines and meticulous attention to detail.

The young woman's demeanour exuded a mix of indifference and amusement. There was a slight curve to her lips, as if she knew something the others didn't. Her expression seemed to convey that she held a secret, a hidden knowledge that set her apart from the rest. There was a certain self-assuredness in her posture, as if she had already anticipated the outcome of the proceedings and was calmly observing the events unfold.

In the room filled with seriousness and tension, the young woman stood out with her enigmatic aura. Her presence demanded attention, and it was clear that she held a significant position within the community. Despite her youth, she carried herself with a sense of authority and confidence that captivated those around her.

As Elizabeth glanced at the young woman, a sense of intrigue washed over her. She couldn't help but wonder about the role this enigmatic figure played in the proceedings and the secrets she might hold. It was as if the young woman embodied the essence of the room itself—an amalgamation of power, mystery, and a hidden agenda.

The disciplinary panel wasted no time in scolding Elizabeth for her impulsive actions, their stern voices echoing through the room. They seemed determined to make their disapproval known, their expressions etched with a combination of disappointment and authority. The atmosphere became charged with tension as they continued to reprimand her, not allowing her a moment to defend herself or explain her intentions.

Their words rang harshly in Elizabeth's ears, each syllable a reminder of her missteps and the consequences she would have to face. The panel members leaned forward slightly, their postures displaying a commanding presence as they addressed her with an unwavering gaze. The room itself seemed to hold its breath, as if waiting for Elizabeth's response.

Despite her mounting desire to explain herself, to present her side of the story, she was met with a wall of silence. The panel showed no signs of yielding, their expressions unyielding and their voices resolute. It felt as though they had already made up their minds, ready to deliver their verdict without considering her perspective.

Elizabeth's frustration grew, the injustice of the situation weighing heavily upon her. She longed to have a voice, to defend her actions, but it seemed that the disciplinary panel was not interested in hearing her side of the story. The scolding continued, their words washing over her like a torrential downpour, leaving her feeling helpless and unheard.

Throughout the ordeal, the young woman with the short blonde haircut maintained her enigmatic expression, her crimson lips slightly upturned in a knowing smile. It was as if she had anticipated this outcome as if she had predicted the panel's response. Her presence added an additional layer of unease, her silence speaking volumes about her position and influence within the disciplinary community.

Elizabeth couldn't help but feel a growing sense of injustice. The panel's refusal to grant her an opportunity to explain herself. All she heard was 'incompetent', 'unprofessional', and 'impulsive'.

'The panel has made the decision to be subject to Agent Emily Martinez right here.' Elizabeth turned to look at the blonde woman who returned her look. So this was the Emily Martinez Joshua told her about.

However, Elizabeth's demotion to be subjected to Emily Martinez, the enigmatic woman in the room, left a bitter taste in her mouth. The realization that she would not only have to work with Martinez but also be under her authority was disheartening. It was clear that Martinez held a position of power within the organization, and the thought of being subjected to her filled Elizabeth with a sense of unease and apprehension.

As the disciplinary panel announced their decision, Elizabeth couldn't help but feel a wave of disappointment wash over her. She argued for a chance to redeem herself, to prove her capabilities and dedication to the organization. However, the panel's decision was fixed. And now she was to be placed under the supervision of Martinez, someone she hardly knew.

The prospect of working under Martinez added a new layer of complexity to Elizabeth's mission. She had never been one to easily trust others, and the circumstances surrounding her demotion only deepened her scepticism. The thought of being subjected to Martinez's leadership and guidance left Elizabeth with a mix of apprehension and curiosity.

As soon as the meeting was over, Elizabeth's anger and frustration mounted as she stormed out of the S.I.S headquarters. The encounter with the mysterious taxi man who knew her name only added to her already heightened emotions. She got out of the building and saw him outside again. She watched as he stood outside the office, his gaze fixed upon her, seemingly unaffected by the authority of the organization.

Driven by curiosity and a sense of urgency, Elizabeth made her way towards the taxi man, hoping to get some answers or at least some clues about his identity. However, as she approached, he abruptly turned and stormed off, leaving Elizabeth standing there, perplexed and with a growing determination to uncover the truth.

Without hesitation, Elizabeth quickly took out a pen and a small notepad from her bag. She noted down the taxi man's plate number. As she scribbled down the details, her mind raced with questions. Who was this taxi man? How did he know her name? And why did he appear so bold and unfazed in the presence of the S.I.S?

With the plate number in hand, Elizabeth knew that she had to find out more about the owner of the taxi and their possible connection to the enigmatic world she found herself tangled in. It was a lead, a small thread that she could follow in her quest to unravel the mysteries surrounding David Scarlett and her own involvement in the web of espionage.

As she stood there in front of the headquarters, Emily Martinez, with a cigarette held casually between her fingers, approached Elizabeth in the S.I.S headquarters. As she drew closer, she extended a cigarette towards Elizabeth, a nonchalant gesture that seemed to reflect her bold and unconventional personality.

Elizabeth, however, declined the offer. The refusal was met with a brief flicker of amusement in Emily's eyes, as if she had expected such a response.

The air around them seemed to crackle with an unspoken tension. Elizabeth sensed that Emily was not just an ordinary agent; there was an intriguing enigma about her. The daredevil grin on Emily's face hinted at a life lived on the edge, unafraid to challenge the status quo and take risks. It was as if she revelled in the excitement of danger and the thrill of breaking the rules.

As the moment lingered between them, Elizabeth couldn't help but feel a curious mix of fascination and wariness towards Emily. She knew she could not fight the fact that their path had converged, and that Emily would play a significant role in her future endeavours within the S.I.S. Yet, the thought of a demotion to this stranger was no good boost to her ego

As Emily took a drag from her cigarette, Elizabeth took a closer look at Emily Martinez, she realized that her initial perception of her age had been mistaken. Emily was not a young woman as she had assumed, but rather a seasoned agent who appeared to be in her early forties. The passing of time had etched a few lines of age beneath her eyes, revealing the experiences and challenges she had faced throughout her career.

Yet, despite the visible signs of age, Emily exuded a sense of strength and resilience. Her gaze held a spark of determination and wisdom that could only come from years of navigating the treacherous waters of intelligence operations. The lines around her eyes told a story of someone who had seen it all, someone who had weathered storms and emerged stronger on the other side.

Emily sighed, her voice tinged with frustration, "The S.I.S. has a knack for throwing a surplus of agents into a mission, as if we're chasing after a ghost from the past," Emily said, her voice laced with discontent. "It feels excessive, as if they're trying to compensate for something or create a show of force that is unnecessary."

She continued, her tone reflecting a critical assessment of the agency's strategy. "Such a heavy-handed approach often leads to confusion, lack of coordination, and compromised operations. We need precision, not an overwhelming number of agents stepping on each other's toes."

"We don't need an army; we need a select few who can work together seamlessly to uncover the truth and bring down the threat at hand." Emily emphasized, her eyes narrowing with determination.

Emily's words hung in the air, carrying a certain weight and intrigue. Her tone of apparent indifference belied a deeper meaning, as if she held a secret that she was reluctant to fully divulge. She turned to Elizabeth, her eyes piercing, and spoke with a mix of caution and wisdom.

"If you want to catch a slithering green snake-like David Scarlett, you have to become one yourself," Emily said, her voice low and measured. She walked away almost immediately as she finished her statement.

Elizabeth stood still there, her mind buzzing with thoughts and questions. She couldn't shake off the feeling that there was more to this case than met the eye. The presence of numerous agents on the hunt for David Scarlett puzzled her. The S.I.S. was renowned for its power and influence, capable of handling even the most elusive targets.

So why the desperate act of sending so many agents to hunt Scarlett?

The more Elizabeth thought about it, the more she realized that Scarlett must possess something of significant value or possess a level of influence that warranted such attention. It wasn't just about catching a criminal; it was about unraveling a much deeper mystery, one that had captured the attention of powerful entities.

The revelation left Elizabeth with a mix of curiosity and caution. She knew she needed to tread carefully, for the stakes were high, and the consequences of missteps could be dire. The fact that Emily had alluded to the need for them to become like snakes themselves further confirmed her suspicions. They were about to enter a dangerous game, where trust would be scarce, and every move needed to be calculated.

As she watched Emily walk away, Elizabeth couldn't help but feel a sense of admiration for her. There was something about Emily's enigmatic demeanour that hinted at a wealth of experience and knowledge. She had seen things, navigated treacherous waters, and survived.

At that moment, she remember Hugh and ran to the street to take a cab to his office.

Elizabeth walked into Hugh's office, finding him deeply engrossed in his work. Papers were scattered across his desk, and he was furiously scribbling notes and signing documents. She could sense his frustration and anger, which hung heavily in the air.

Elizabeth stood in silence as Hugh continued to write, his attention solely focused on the documents in front of him. She felt a mix of disappointment and frustration at his lack of response.

"Hugh," she called out, her voice slightly hesitant. But Hugh continued with his paper works, refusing to acknowledge her "Hugh," she spoke up again, her voice firmer this time, "I need your help. This is important."

Still, Hugh remained engrossed in his work, refusing to acknowledge her. Elizabeth's frustration grew, but she refused to be deterred. She walked closer to his desk, determined to get his attention.

"Hugh, please," she pleaded, her voice tinged with desperation. "Look, I know

I made a mistake, but I need your support. I can't let David Scarlett slip away."

Finally, after what felt like an eternity, Hugh paused and slowly raised his eyes to meet Elizabeth's gaze. There was a hint of annoyance in his expression.

"What is it, Elizabeth?" he asked, his voice tinged with irritation.

"Hugh, I want to apologize for my actions," she began, her voice filled with remorse. "I know I acted recklessly, and I let my emotions get the better of me. It was not fair to you or our partnership, and I deeply regret it."

Hugh raised his head again and looked directly at Elizabeth, his eyes filled with a mix of frustration and concern. He sighed heavily before speaking, his voice filled with a mixture of disappointment and worry.

"What were you thinking, Elizabeth?" he asked, his tone conveyed frustration "Your impulsive actions almost cost me my job. We're dealing with highly sensitive operations here, and your unauthorized actions put everything at risk."

"I'm so sorry, Hugh," she replied, her voice filled with remorse. "I didn't think about the consequences, and I never meant to put you in jeopardy. I was just so focused on finding answers and getting to the truth.'

It struck Elizabeth at that moment that Hugh might have more discreet information regarding Crane and potentially even more valuable insights into David Scarlett's organization. This thought filled her with a sense of hope and anticipation, igniting a glimmer of happiness within her.

"Hugh," she continued, her voice filled with a mix of humility and determination, "I know I've made mistakes, and I'm truly sorry for my impulsive actions. But I also believe that we can still work together to bring David Scarlett to justice. The information you gave me earlier went a long way, and I can't help but hope you might have more insights or resources that could assist me in this investigation?"

"Elizabeth," he began, his voice measured, "I appreciate your apology and your willingness to make things right. I do have access to additional information that might aid you in our pursuit of David Scarlett. However, there's no way I'm getting it out to anybody, not to talk of you."

Elizabeth felt frustration bubbling inside her. She couldn't understand why he was being so stubborn and withholding crucial details from her.

"Why are you doing this, Hugh?" Elizabeth exclaimed, her voice trembling with a mixture of anger and desperation. "I thought you were my friend, someone I could trust. But here you are, keeping vital information from me."

Hugh leaned back in his chair, his expression firm and resolute. "Elizabeth, you need to understand that there are protocols and procedures in place for a reason. You can't just go around acting on your own accord, especially when it puts yourself and others in danger."

"But this is personal, Hugh!" Elizabeth shot back, her eyes brimming. 'I could lose everything if I don't sort this one out.'

Hugh's eyes remained firm and cold. "I understand your pain, Elizabeth. But emotions cloud judgment, and you need to think logically. Acting on your own will only put you in more danger. Trust the process, trust the system."

Elizabeth clenched her fists, 'what the fuck are you saying, Hugh. System? Really? You mean the system that took my dad and never stood up for him in death. That one?'

Hugh stood up abruptly, his voice filled with a stern authority. "No, Elizabeth.

You need to listen to me. You have a superior now, and you need to obey their instructions. They will guide you and provide the resources you need. Going against their directives will only make things worse."

As the argument escalated, Hugh and Elizabeth unleashing their pent-up frustrations and grievances. The air became charged with tension as harsh words were exchanged, and their voices dripped with accusation and resentment.

"You've always been this way, Elizabeth," Hugh retorted, his voice tinged with exasperation. "You've never been able to trust anyone in authority, always thinking you know better than the rest of us. It's your arrogance that blinds you to the importance of following rules and protocols."

Elizabeth's eyes narrowed, a flash of anger crossing her face. "Arrogance? No, Hugh, it's called questioning the system that has failed us time and time again. Blindly following rules won't lead us anywhere. You, my friend, need to think outside the box, take risks, and challenge the status quo."

'My God, Liz, why do you love to self-destruct!'

Elizabeth chuckled 'I don't, Hugh. I'm just not a coward. You, on the other hand, you're just a coward, Hugh," Elizabeth spat, her voice laced with disdain. "You're so afraid of taking risks that you've become a puppet of the system. Following orders like a mindless drone won't bring justice. It's about time someone shook things up."

Hugh's jaw clenched, his face turning red with anger. "And what about the consequences, Elizabeth? What about the innocent lives that could be endangered by your reckless pursuit? You're so blinded by ambition that you're willing to throw everything away."

The room seemed to grow smaller as their words echoed, reverberating with the weight of their emotions. Their once-strong bond appeared to fracture under the strain of the argument, leaving them standing on opposite sides of a widening divide.

When Elizabeth couldn't take it anymore, she stormed out of Hugh's office, determined to figure out another way out without his help.

While walking across the street, Elizabeth's phone rang and she answered the call from Emily. Emily's voice was brisk and business-like, wasting no time on pleasantries.

"Elizabeth, we're leaving for Germany tomorrow," Emily said, her tone firm and direct. "We've received information that David Scarlett has some open tracks there, and we need to act quickly."

Elizabeth felt a surge of mixed emotions. On one hand, she was relieved to have a new lead and a chance to continue her pursuit of David Scarlett. On the other hand, she couldn't shake off the disappointment of the unresolved argument with Hugh.

Nevertheless, she knew that she had to put her personal feelings aside and focus on the task at hand.

"Alright, Emily," Elizabeth replied, her voice composed. "I'm ready. Where and when do we meet?"

Emily provided her with the necessary details, instructing Elizabeth to gather her belongings and meet her at a designated location early the next morning. The conversation ended abruptly, leaving Elizabeth to process the information and make the necessary preparations.

That moment Elizabeth realised she had not said hello to her Nana and she would be leaving London soon.

Elizabeth hailed a taxi and gave the driver directions to her grandmother's house. As they weaved through the streets of London, Elizabeth's thoughts wandered to her beloved Nana. She hadn't seen her in a while, and she knew that a visit would bring her some comfort amidst the chaos of her current situation.

The taxi pulled up to a charming apartment building in a quiet neighbourhood. Elizabeth paid the driver and stepped out onto the cobblestone street. She made her way to the entrance of the building, a well-maintained structure that exuded an old-world charm.

The front door opened with a slight creak, revealing a small foyer adorned with patterned wallpaper and a vintage chandelier hanging from the ceiling. The scent of lavender filled the air, a favourite fragrance of her grandmother. Elizabeth's footsteps echoed softly as she made her way up the staircase, the wooden bannister worn with age but polished to a shine.

Reaching the second floor, Elizabeth turned left and arrived at her grandmother's door. She paused for a moment, taking in the sight of the apartment. It was like stepping back in time, a true reflection of the 1950s era.

The door opened, revealing her Nana, who looked really happy to see Elizabeth. Her grandmother's apartment was cosy and inviting, with a warm colour palette of pastel blues and pinks. The furniture was elegant yet comfortable, with plush armchairs and a vintage sofa adorned with embroidered cushions. A fireplace stood as the centrepiece of the living room, its mantel adorned with cherished family photographs.

The walls were adorned with delicate floral wallpaper, adding a touch of femininity to the space. Antique wooden cabinets lined one side of the room, showcasing delicate china and heirloom teacups. A small radio sat on a nearby table, softly playing tunes from the era.

In the corner, a record player stood, ready to spin nostalgic melodies. Elizabeth recalled fond memories of dancing with her Nana to the tunes of Frank Sinatra and Ella Fitzgerald.

The apartment had a timeless charm, with lace curtains framing the windows, allowing soft sunlight to filter in. The floors were covered with a plush carpet that harkened back to a bygone era. Elizabeth could almost hear the faint echo of laughter and conversations from the past, bringing a sense of nostalgia and comfort.

As Elizabeth embraced her Nana, she couldn't help but feel a sense of grounding and solace in the familiar surroundings. Her grandmother's apartment was a haven, a sanctuary from the uncertainties of the outside world.

They spent the afternoon reminiscing, sipping tea from delicate china cups, and sharing stories of family and love. In that moment, surrounded by the beauty of the 1950s London apartment and the warmth of her grandmother's embrace, Elizabeth found a temporary respite from the challenges that awaited her in the days to come.

As Elizabeth and her Nana sat in the cosy living room of the 1950s London apartment, sipping tea and exchanging stories, the conversation took an unexpected turn. Nana's gentle eyes carried a hint of sadness as she broached the topic of Elizabeth's father, a subject that always stirred a mix of emotions within her.

Nana, with her silver hair styled in a classic updo, sat in her favourite armchair across from Elizabeth. The sunlight streaming through the lace curtains cast a soft glow on the room, creating an atmosphere of intimacy and trust.

"Elizabeth, my dear," Nana began, her voice tinged with both affection and concern. "I know we don't speak much about your father, and it's been a sensitive subject for you. But there are things I believe you should know."

Elizabeth shifted in her seat, her unease palpable. She had always felt a void when it came to her father, his absence leaving unanswered questions that lingered deep within her. Though part of her yearned to uncover the truth, another part feared the painful revelations that might arise.

Nana reached out and gently clasped Elizabeth's hand, her touch warm and reassuring. "Your father was a complex man, Elizabeth. He had his flaws, but he loved you dearly. Circumstances pulled him away, and his choices were not always easy or honourable. But he carried a burden that haunted him until the end."

Elizabeth's eyes welled up with tears, a mixture of frustration, curiosity, and longing. She had spent years wondering about her father, piecing together fragmented stories and searching for any traces of his existence.

While Nana talked, Elizabeth thought about her father's heroic acts and untimely death, she felt a mix of pride, sorrow, and determination. She had grown up knowing the story of her father's bravery and sacrifice, and it had shaped her own sense of purpose.

Sitting in the comfortable armchair, Elizabeth closed her eyes and let her thoughts drift. She recalled the stories her mother had shared, the fragments of memories and whispered conversations that had painted a picture of a man dedicated to his country and the safety of its people.

Her father's death, shrouded in mystery, had always been a lingering question in her mind. The assassination of a man who had thwarted an attempt on the lives of prominent figures, including the Prime Minister and a member of the royal family, remained an unsolved puzzle.

As Elizabeth left her grandmother's apartment, that evening, she made a conscious decision to push aside the painful memories of her father's death. While his legacy inspired her, she knew that dwelling on the past would not serve her in her quest to find David Scarlett.

Instead, she focused on cultivating a sense of inner strength and determination. She knew that to uncover the truth and track down an elusive figure like David Scarlett, she would need to rely on her own skills, instincts, and resourcefulness.

As she walked through the bustling streets of London, Elizabeth felt a surge of empowerment. She knew that relying solely on herself would demand immense effort and perseverance, but she embraced the challenge. She would not be deterred by the complexities of the task or the dangers that lay ahead. She was determined to confront David Scarlett and uncover the truth, no matter the obstacles.

CHAPTER FIVE: PURSUIT ACROSS BORDERS.

As Elizabeth and Emily stepped foot in Germany. The streets bustled with activity, and the air was filled with a sense of energy and excitement. It was a city that seamlessly blended the old and the new, where history intertwined with modernity.

Gothic spires reached towards the sky, adorning cathedrals and churches, while Baroque facades adorned grand palaces and government buildings. The streets were lined with charming half-timbered houses, their ornate details reflecting the craftsmanship of a bygone era. As Elizabeth and Emily wandered through the city, they couldn't help but marvel at the intricate carvings, elaborate facades, and meticulous attention to detail that adorned the buildings.

As they made their way through the streets of Germany, Emily began sharing more details about their next location. There would be heading to the mansion of a man named Reinhardt. Emily explained Reinhardt and his connections to the world of espionage.

Reinhardt's shadowy past was shrouded in mystery and intrigue. Born during a tumultuous era, he had once been a Soviet spy, operating in the shadows and carrying out covert missions for the intelligence agency. His skills in deception, manipulation, and information gathering made him a formidable asset to the Soviets, earning him a reputation as a cunning and resourceful operative.

'He was formerly known as the devil himself because of his ruthlessness when it came to his operation in the world of espionage. Towards the later end of his life, he was exposed by Mason Morgan, your father and took to his heel, leaving his networks behind.'

They walked briskly, their footsteps echoing against the cobblestone pavement. The city bustled around them, with people going about their daily lives, their attire a mix of traditional and modern styles.

Emily, her voice laced with a sense of urgency as she talked about Reinhardt as a shadowy figure with a complex past. She mentioned his involvement with intelligence agencies, his reputation as a master manipulator, and his suspected ties to David Scarlett. Elizabeth listened intently, her mind racing with questions and possibilities.

'Reinhardt eventually surrendered when he was on in his hideout in South Africa. He agreed to be a double agent, leaking information from the already Soviet forces to the West.'

After his death, rumours of Reinhardt's association with David Scarlett swirled through the intelligence community.

It was understandable for people like Reinhardt to be associated with David Scarlett. The intelligence agencies had been pursuing Reinhardt and Scarlett for years, their paths intertwining in a web of secrets and deceit. They were elusive figures, masterminds of manipulation and espionage, capable of infiltrating the highest echelons of power. Their connection was a puzzle that needed to be solved, a key to unlocking the secrets of a complex and dangerous world, Elizabeth thought.

'Was he killed?' Elizabeth asked

'No, he was murdered. No one knows who did, and no one cared.'

Her mind wondered if Reinhardt could be responsible for her father's death, since he was responsible for exposing him. 'So what connection does Reinhardt have with David Scarlett?' Elizabeth asked.

'You didn't read the briefing I sent you, did you?' Emily furrowed her eyebrow.

'He has a nose for the underworld. Report has it that he had more than an interaction with David Scarlett. They might have served in espionage together.'

Emily hurried her steps leaving Elizabeth behind to piece these information together. As the streets buzzed with the hum of traffic, the occasional clatter of a tram passing by, and snippets of conversations in different languages. Elizabeth's anticipation grew with each step, knowing that they were getting closer to Reinhardt's mansion and the secrets it held. It was thrilling to know that there was not just a connection between Reinhardt and David Scarlett but also a connection between Reinhardt and her father.

As they rounded a corner, the imposing gates of Reinhardt's estate came into view. The mansion loomed in the distance, its presence commanding attention and stirring a mix

Reinhardt's mansion, a fortress of secrets and hidden agendas, stood as a physical manifestation of his enigmatic persona. Its grandeur and imposing presence mirrored the complexity of the man himself.

As Elizabeth and Emily approached Reinhardt's mansion, they were met by an imposing figure standing at the entrance. It was the maid, an old woman with a commanding presence that seemed to fill the air around her. Her tall stature and strong build were a testament to a life of hard work and resilience.

The maid had long, flowing blonde hair that cascaded down her back in gentle waves. It was a stark contrast to her stern expression, which seemed to carry an air of authority and an unyielding determination. Her eyes, piercing and sharp, held a gaze that could penetrate the deepest secrets, like a hawk surveilling its prey.

She stood tall and upright, her posture impeccable. Her piercing gaze, like that of a predator assessing its prey, bore into Elizabeth's soul. The intensity of her eyes held a world of untold stories, a depth of experience that seemed to hint at a life lived on the edge.

Her face, weathered by time and marked by lines of wisdom, displayed an unwavering resolve. A strong jawline and sharp cheekbones gave her a regal air, while a stern expression etched across her features added an element of strictness to her countenance. It was a face that commanded respect, demanding obedience and loyalty.

The maid's presence was further accentuated by her choice of attire. She wore a traditional black dress, its fabric clinging to her frame, emphasizing her strength and presence. The dress was perfectly tailored, emphasizing her imposing stature. Every movement she made seemed deliberate, purposeful, as if she had complete control over her surroundings.

Her posture, combined with the way she carried herself, exuded a sense of dominance. It was as if she had mastered the art of commanding respect through her mere presence. The way she held herself spoke volumes, suggesting that she was not one to be crossed or underestimated.

One aspect that caught Elizabeth's attention was the maid's large and ample bosom and her feet. They were surprisingly small, almost delicate, as if they belonged to a completely different person. The contrast between her towering figure and those petite feet was both intriguing and disconcerting. It was as if she possessed a duality, embodying strength and grace in equal measure.

There was an aura of mystery surrounding the maid, as if she held a wealth of knowledge and secrets within the confines of the mansion. She was more than just a servant; she was a guardian of the mansion's history and the stories that unfolded within its walls. Her intimidating glare and imposing stature made it clear that she was not to be underestimated.

In the silence that followed, Elizabeth couldn't help but wonder about the depths of the maid's power and the secrets she held. Elizabeth couldn't help but feel a mix of apprehension and awe in the presence of this formidable woman,

Emily stepped forward and spoke to the maid in fluent German, engaging in a brief exchange that Elizabeth couldn't quite follow. The conversation seem polite, and the sharp gaze on the maid soften a little as the conversation proceeded. As the conversation concluded, the maid's sharp gaze resumed, and this time it shifted from Emily to Elizabeth, and a palpable tension filled the air. Her eyes bore into Elizabeth's with an intensity that seemed to convey a deep-seated disapproval.

Elizabeth felt the weight of the maid's scrutiny, her penetrating stare leaving her feeling exposed and vulnerable. It was as if the maid saw through her, reading her intentions and questioning her presence within the mansion's hallowed halls. The disdain in her eyes was unmistakable, a silent challenge that Elizabeth was determined to face head-on.

The maid's disapproving gaze lingered on Elizabeth as she reluctantly motioned for them to enter the mansion. There was a distinct coldness in her demeanour, a subtle indication that she did not extend her hospitality willingly. Elizabeth couldn't help but wonder what had caused this animosity, what preconceived notions or judgments the maid had formed about her.

Reinhardt's mansion stood as a formidable structure, exuding an aura of gothic grandeur and mystery. As Elizabeth and Emily stepped through its imposing iron gates, they found themselves in the presence of an architectural marvel that seemed frozen in time.

The mansion rose high, its darkened stone façade reaching towards the heavens. Tall, narrow windows adorned its exterior, their intricate tracery casting long shadows on the surrounding grounds. The building's silhouette was imposing, with turrets and spires that reached towards the sky like the fingers of a beckoning spectre.

The entrance to the mansion was guarded by a massive wooden door, its surface carved with intricate patterns that seemed to tell stories of forgotten times. As the door creaked open, revealing the dimly lit interior, an eerie ambience enveloped Elizabeth and Emily.

The walls of the mansion were adorned with faded tapestries depicting scenes from bygone eras, their threads worn with age and hinting at a rich history that had unfolded within these walls. Paintings of sombre-faced ancestors stared down from their gilded frames, their eyes following the visitors as they moved through the rooms.

The mansion's interior was adorned with ornate furnishings that echoed the grandeur of a bygone era. Ancient chandeliers hung from the ceiling, their crystal prisms refracting the feeble candlelight, casting eerie rainbows across the walls. The floors were covered in faded rugs, their patterns worn and frayed, but still hinting at the opulence that once permeated these halls.

The atmosphere within Reinhardt's mansion was tinged with a sense of melancholy and foreboding. The silence that hung in the air seemed to carry whispers of forgotten secrets, as if the very walls of the mansion held a tale waiting to be unravelled. The sound of distant footsteps echoed through the corridors, further enhancing the sense of an unseen presence lingering just beyond sight.

Reinhardt's mansion was a place that seemed to exist outside the realm of ordinary reality, where the lines between the living and the spectral were blurred. Its gothic and eerie aesthetic left an indelible impression on Elizabeth, reminding her that she was treading upon hallowed ground, where the truth she sought might be shrouded in the shadows.

In a corner of Reinhardt's mansion, Elizabeth and Emily stumbled upon an unusual sight that gave them pause. Two giant steel dog food bowls, each the size of a small bathtub, sat side by side on the floor. The sheer scale of these bowls was awe-inspiring, hinting at the presence of formidable creatures that once dined from them.

Above the bowls, a painted portrait commanded attention. It depicted Reinhardt's two menacing German shepherd dogs, capturing their imposing presence and ferocious nature. The artist had expertly captured the intensity in their eyes, which seemed to follow the viewers with an unwavering gaze. The dogs looked with strong, muscular bodies, their sleek fur rendered in a mix of deep browns and blacks, reflecting their power and strength.

The German Shepherds appeared poised and alert, their ears erect and their jaws clenched with an air of authority. Their sharp teeth, glistening white against their dark muzzles, conveyed a sense of danger and unpredictability. The artist's skilful brushwork brought the dogs to life, capturing their innate intensity and creating an almost tangible aura of intimidation.

The backdrop of the portrait added to the atmosphere of foreboding. Dark shades of grey and black dominated, giving the impression of a shadowy environment. The dogs seemed to emerge from this darkness, their fierce expressions contrasting sharply with the muted background, as if they were guardians of a realm hidden from ordinary view.

The presence of the giant steel dog food bowls hinted at the scale and strength of these formidable animals. It was clear that Reinhardt spared no expense in catering to his canine companions, providing them with the sustenance they needed to maintain their imposing stature. The sheer size of the bowls underscored the magnitude of their appetite and the significance they held in Reinhardt's world.

As Elizabeth and Emily stood before the portrait and the colossal dog food bowls, a mix of fascination and trepidation washed over them. It was evident that Reinhardt's German Shepherds were not mere pets but formidable sentinels, fiercely loyal to their master and prepared to defend their territory with unwavering determination.

'Man loves his dogs' Emily said and chuckled as she moved on

Since they stepped into the grand foyer of the mansion, Elizabeth couldn't shake the feeling of being watched. The maid's eyes seemed to follow her every move, her gaze unwavering and filled with suspicion. It was clear that the maid's scepticism ran deep, and Elizabeth knew she would have to prove herself in order to earn her trust and respect.

Throughout their exploration of the mansion, the maid remained a constant presence, her watchful eyes never leaving Elizabeth's form. It seemed as if she was keeping a vigilant eye on her, monitoring her every action and waiting for any misstep or sign of betrayal. Elizabeth could feel the weight of the maid's scrutiny with every step she took, a reminder that her every move was being observed and judged.

Despite the maid's evident disdain, It was clear that she held a deep loyalty to Reinhardt and his legacy, and her protective nature over the mansion's secrets was evident in the way she conducted herself.

Emily and Elizabeth got into Reinhardt's library meticulously sifted through Reinhardt's files and records, while the giant maid was away. They hoped to uncover some clue, some shred of information that would lead them to David Scarlett. However, their search yielded disappointing results. The files contained no direct mention of David Scarlett or any evidence linking Reinhardt to him.

The room they were in was dimly lit, with dusty shelves lined with rows of files that seemed to stretch endlessly. The air carried a musty smell, a testament to the passage of time and the neglected state of the documents. The files themselves were organized in a haphazard manner, making their search all the more challenging.

They painstakingly examined each file, one by one, hoping for a breakthrough. But as they delved deeper into Reinhardt's records, it became apparent that his association with David Scarlett was carefully concealed, shrouded in secrecy. The absence of any direct references or incriminating documents was both frustrating and perplexing.

It was as if Reinhardt had taken great care to erase any trace of his past collaboration with anyone called David Scarlett, leaving behind only fragments and cryptic hints that required further investigation. The files contained information on Reinhardt's past as a Soviet spy, his double-agent status, and other relevant details, but not one connection to anyone called David Scarlett.

As they closed files upon files and set them aside, they realised that their search had revealed more questions than answers.

As Elizabeth's eyes scanned through the disarray of files, her attention was suddenly drawn to a file labelled "Daniel Carter." The name struck a chord within her, resonating with a sense of familiarity. She couldn't shake the feeling that she had come across this name before.

With a surge of adrenaline, Elizabeth carefully and swiftly tucked the file into her jacket, concealing it. There was this strong feeling in her heart that this piece of information could be significant, and she didn't want to risk anyone else discovering it before she had a chance to examine its contents.

As the file felt weighty in her jacket, Elizabeth turned around and saw the maid was back in the library, and her gaze lingered suspiciously upon her. Elizabeth maintained her composure, careful not to reveal any hint of the valuable file she had acquired.

With her heart racing and her mind focused, Elizabeth moved forward and approached Emily, her eyes focused and determination etched on her face. Despite the lingering gaze of the intimidating blonde maid, she pushed the distractions aside, determined to stay focused on their mission.

The maid soon returned back to the shadows where she came from, leaving Emily and Elizabeth alone again.

Emily, engrossed in her search, glanced up as Elizabeth approached. There was a spark of curiosity in her eyes, as if she could sense something had changed. But she turned her head back to her search and continued searching

Elizabeth turned to Emily with a furrowed brow, her voice laced with curiosity and concern.

"Do you know what killed Reinhardt?" she inquired, her tone hushed as if afraid the very walls of the mansion might have ears.

Emily paused for a moment, her gaze was fixed on the file before her, before finally meeting Elizabeth's eyes. "Ricin poison," she said and went back to combing through the files...

"Why Ricin?" Elizabeth asked, her voice betraying a mix of curiosity and apprehension.

Emily's gaze turned distant for a moment, she seem irritated Elizabeth kept asking her questions she could figure out on her own. "Ricin is a message," she replied, her voice tinged with a hint of irritation. "A message that says, 'we are watching, and we can strike at any time.'"

As Emily's words sank in, a flicker of recognition flashed across Elizabeth's face. The mention of Ricin poison triggered a distant memory buried deep within her subconscious. It was a memory of hushed conversations and whispered warnings, a memory of her father speaking to her mother about the dangers they faced in their line of work.

She closed her eyes for a moment, trying to grasp at the fragments of that memory. The image of her father's furrowed brow, the weight of his words as he spoke of colleagues lost to this insidious poison, it all came rushing back to her. Ricin had taken lives before, lives intertwined with her own father's history.

A sense of unease settled over Elizabeth, mingling with her determination to uncover the truth behind David Scarlett. The poison that had claimed the lives of her father's colleagues now resurfaced in the midst of her own investigation.

She took a deep breath, pushing aside the unsettling memories. Elizabeth knew she couldn't let fear or doubt deter her from her mission.

Emily raised a file up and smiled. She seem to have found something she required and was happy about it. 'It's very interesting that Reinhardt, once a Soviet spy turned double agent, had met his demise through a method that bore the unmistakable hallmark of the shadowy world they were delving into.' Emily brought out her device and quickly scanned the document before the old maiden made her way into the room.

As Elizabeth's mind raced with thoughts and fragments of information, a pattern began to form in her thoughts. She couldn't ignore the nagging feeling that there was a connection between her father, Mason Morgan, Daniel Carter, and Reinhardt. It was an intuitive leap, a hunch born out of the pieces of the puzzle scattered before her.

She pondered the possibilities, considering the threads that linked these individuals together. Her father's involvement in uncovering spy agents, Daniel Carter's familiar name, and now the presence of Reinhardt, a former Soviet spy turned double agent.

Elizabeth's analytical mind went into overdrive, seeking patterns, and searching for hidden connections. She knew that her instincts had led her down unexpected paths before, and they couldn't be dismissed lightly. There was something more at play, something that tied these figures together in ways she was only beginning to comprehend.

These strange vacuum she seeks could be the key to finally unveiling who David Scarlett is.

Elizabeth looked back at Emily, who looked happy to discover the new file that may or may not add significance to the case. She thought of telling her these things she thought. But she also recognized the need for caution. Speculation alone wouldn't provide concrete answers. She needed evidence, and facts to support her growing suspicions. It was a delicate balance between following her intuition and maintaining a rational approach to her investigation.

As Elizabeth's thoughts swirled with the weight of the dark secrets she believed lay beneath the surface, she couldn't bring herself to share her inner musings with Emily just yet. Not only did she understand the gravity of the information she was piecing together, and she felt the need to tread cautiously. But she still thinks Emily is an arrogant bitch that wants all the credit for herself.

The investigation had already revealed glimpses of a complex web of connections, and Elizabeth knew that delving further into these secrets would require her to confront deeper truths.

At the moment, there are seem to be the possibility of powerful forces at play, hidden agendas, and hidden hands pulling the strings from the shadows. Revealing her suspicions prematurely could jeopardise not only her investigation but also her safety.

She needed to gather solid evidence, build a strong foundation before presenting her findings to her superiors. Elizabeth was aware that her thoughts and theories needed to be grounded in tangible proof if she wanted to be taken seriously and avoid unnecessary risks.

CHAPTER SIX: THE EXOTIC SHOW-DOWN

Inside the aeroplane, Elizabeth and Emily settled into their seats, ready for their journey to Brazil. Elizabeth observed Emily engrossed in her laptop, likely typing up a report on their findings at Reinhardt's mansion. Her fingers moved swiftly across the keys, tapping with purpose as she meticulously documented their progress in uncovering information about David Scarlett. A progress Elizabeth is yet to be informed of. And a progress Emily only intends to take credit for all by herself.

Elizabeth could see the determination in Emily's expression, her focus unyielding as she took her role seriously. The soft glow of the phone illuminated Emily's features, casting a faint light on her face. Her brows furrowed slightly, hinting at the weight of the task at hand.

As Emily continued to type, Elizabeth's mind raced with thoughts and questions. She wondered how they could proceed without any solid leads on David Scarlett. The enigma surrounding him seemed impenetrable, leaving them grasping at straws in their pursuit of the truth.

She glanced out of the window, the vast expanse of the sky stretching out before her. The journey to Brazil seemed to hold a glimmer of hope, an opportunity to dig deeper and unravel the threads of this intricate web they found themselves entangled in.

After a while, Emily finished her report and looked up from her phone. Their eyes met, and Elizabeth could see a mixture of frustration and determination in Emily's gaze. It was clear that her report got bounced. Elizabeth had no idea. But they had hardly gotten any time to rest for the past few days.

It had been 2 hours of flight, and the silence between both ladies persisted. Elizabeth was not sure if this was deliberate on Emily's side. Perhaps she felt there was nothing of interest in Elizabeth except when it was time for work, or she just didn't have anything to say to her.

Elizabeth took a deep breath and gathered her thoughts before breaking the awkward silence that had settled between them during the flight. She turned to Emily,

"Emily,'

'Yes?' Emily answered with her gaze out the window.

'What did you mean by what you mentioned earlier when you said that to catch a slithering green snake like David Scarlett, I might have to become one myself.'

Emily paused for a moment, her gaze shifting from the window to Elizabeth. She seemed to contemplate her response, as if carefully as if she was thinking of the most simplistic terms she could use to convert her words.

"In order to outsmart and apprehend someone like David Scarlett, you might have to opt for unconventional methods, we have to think like the person we are pursuing, to understand their motives, their strategies, and their vulnerabilities. By becoming a 'green slithering snake,' I mean being willing to delve into the shadows, to navigate the murky waters'

Elizabeth listened intently, surprised by her interest in Emily's words.

Emily continued, her voice steady, "Just as a snake would. We must be willing to adapt, to shed our old skin and take on new identities, if necessary, to gain the upper hand. It's about thinking outside the box, using every tool at our disposal to infiltrate his world and expose his true nature."

Emily leaned back in her seat, a nostalgic smile playing on her lips as she recounted her past experience to Elizabeth. She started with her experiences as a young agent, she had learned to utilise her feminine advantage to gain an upper hand in a case. 'It was a delicate balance of strategy, observation, and exploiting the weaknesses of my targets.' Emily said proudly

She recalled a specific case where she had been tasked with gathering evidence from a key witness, a man known for his questionable behaviour and perversion. Emily described how she meticulously studied her prey, observing his actions, tendencies, and vulnerabilities.

'He's a perverted bitch, that one. In a moment of calculated brilliance, I identified his moment of weakness and seized the opportunity to get him coughing information up. With precision and finesse, I struck him off guard and left him defenceless.' She described the satisfaction she felt as she watched him crumble under the weight of his own actions, realising he had been outmanoeuvred by an ordinary woman...

Emily continued, to Elizabeth's interest and slight discomfort. It was quite interesting to see the quiet, enigmatic figure transform into a loquacious yapping person that loved herself so much.

As Emily shared her story, her voice carried a sense of pride and confidence. She spoke of it as a testament to her abilities as an agent, highlighting the resourcefulness and adaptability required to navigate the complexities of her line of work. It was clear that she had honed her skills over the years and had come to embrace her own unique approach to achieving her goals.

Emily shared accounts of high-stakes operations, where her quick thinking and combat prowess had turned the tides in her favour. She spoke of daring infiltrations, strategic takedowns, and narrow escapes from dangerous situations. Her words painted vivid pictures of action-packed missions, leaving Elizabeth on the edge of her seat, mentally visualizing each scene.

With each story, Emily revealed a new facet of her skill set. She showcased her ability to blend seamlessly into different environments, adopting various disguises and personas to gain crucial information. Her resourcefulness and adaptability shone through as she described navigating treacherous terrains, deciphering complex codes, and outsmarting formidable opponents.

Elizabeth listened intently, absorbing Emily's words and reflecting on Elizabeth's approaches. While Emily's expertise has been a successful one and the results she had achieved celebrated, Elizabeth wondered if the ethical implications of such tactics were justifiable.

She concluded that Emily was quite the manipulative type who would do anything to get her ambition. But wasn't she just like her? A thought rang in Elizabeth's mind. Was she not willing to sell her friends out because she wanted a promotion? She thought of Hugh at that moment and the pain she must have caused him in blowing up Crane's case.

To erase the weight of guilt she felt at that moment, she decided to engage Emily

'How did you manage to learn such diverse skills?' Elizabeth asked almost absentmindedly

'Well, being an agent requires more than just physical and combat training. It demands adaptability and the ability to blend into various situations. So, over the years, I've learned to acquire different skills to aid me in my missions.' Elizabeth said with a proud smile on her face.

'Hmm, Skill, eh?'

'Yes. One time, I needed to infiltrate an espionage operation disguised as a musician. So, I learned to play the flute proficiently. I played a concert. Could you believe that?' Emily smiled proudly. 'It allowed me to gain access to a high-security event where I was able to gather critical information without arousing suspicion.'

'That's quite unexpected,' Elizabeth muttered jealously. The only skills she had acquired on her own journey was being a ballerina. And this was easy for her to walk through because she had been practising since she was little.

'Well, here's one that might surprise you. I learned the art of belly dancing.'

Elizabeth raised a very high sceptical eyebrow. 'Belly dancing? Really? I find that hard to believe, considering your...well...' Elizabeth wanted to say her uptightness, but that would be rude

'Oh, believe me, it's all about the element of surprise.' Emily said, grinning. 'Belly dancing allowed me to infiltrate certain social circles and gatherings where key individuals held crucial information. It was quite effective in disarming potential threats and gaining their trust.'

'Well, I need to start taking my job too seriously' Elizabeth turned away and said to herself

But Emily heard her 'Absolutely, Elizabeth.' she nodded her head, ignoring the sarcasm 'In this line of work, we must be willing to adapt and learn whatever skills are necessary to accomplish our mission objectives. It's all about staying one step ahead and using every tool at our disposal.'

Elizabeth turned back to Emily, seeing she was still interested in the conversation

'So, Emily, do you have any plans on how we'll go about finding David Scarlett once we reach Brazil?'

Emily smirked 'Well, Elizabeth, my plan is always no plan.'

Elizabeth looked at her, surprised 'No plan? Isn't that reckless?'

Emily sighed satisfactorily and leaned back in her seat 'Not at all, my dear. You see, when you have a specific plan, it leaves little room for flexibility. In this line of work, adaptability is key. We must be able to think on our feet and adjust our approach based on the ever-changing circumstances.

Elizabeth rolled her eyes and muttered under her breath, 'Tell me more of what I don't need to know'

Emily turned, catching Elizabeth's muttering, 'Excuse me?'

'Oh, nothing. I just find it interesting that you prefer to operate without a plan. It's just... quite different from the status quo, isn't it?'

Emily chuckled slightly. 'You didn't have a plan when you busted into Crane's shop, did you? Speaking of not following the status quo?'

There was an immediate silence between them.

Elizabeth's mind wandered as she contemplated Emily's approach to their mission. While she understood the value of adaptability and seizing opportunities, she couldn't shake off the feeling that Emily was acting independently, almost as if she had her own agenda.

However, Elizabeth was determined to stay one step ahead. She had her own theories and leads that she hadn't shared with Emily. Elizabeth believed with thorough research, meticulous planning, and she could focus on the target and not slide into the mistake she made at Crane's shop again.

A few hours before they arrive in Brazil, Emily finally broke the awkward silence. She reached into her bag and pulled out a file. With a calculated glance, she handed it to Elizabeth, who took it, her eyes scanning the cover. The file was labelled "Peter Bashir - Operation Nightfall." It was a thick dossier filled with photographs, reports, and classified information.

Emily leaned in closer to Elizabeth, their faces illuminated by the soft glow of the cabin lights. Her voice lowered, ensuring their conversation remained private amidst the hum of the engines.

"Peter Bashir is a key to unravelling the mystery surrounding David Scarlett," Emily began, "He was once a notorious figure in the underworld, operating a high-end brothel in the heart of Brazil. But now, he has reinvented himself as a club owner, providing the perfect cover for his connections and activities.

He has changed his name over eleven times over the years, keeping only his initials through it all"

Elizabeth flipped through the pages of the file, scanning photographs of Peter Bashir and the club he owned. The images captured a man with a charismatic aura, his eyes betraying the secrets he held.

"Our intelligence community has reason to believe that Peter Bashir had ties to the Soviet intelligence network in the past," Emily continued. "He may have worked alongside David Scarlett, sharing information, resources, and possibly even carrying out joint operations."

Elizabeth's mind raced with possibilities. This was a new character in the already complex and complicated case she had at hand.

"Our mission in Brazil is to gain Bashir's trust and extract any information he has on David Scarlett," Emily explained. "We need to approach him carefully, earn his confidence, and ensure he doesn't suspect our true intentions. We must be prepared for anything, as Bashir is known for his shrewdness and cunning."

Elizabeth nodded, as she flipped through the files.

"We'll need to blend in with the club scene, become a part of Bashir's world," Emily emphasised. "We'll gather intelligence, observe, and exploit any weaknesses or vulnerabilities we discover. Our ultimate goal is to force Bashir's hand, to make him reveal what he knows about David Scarlett."

Elizabeth carefully examined the photograph of Peter Bashir, studying his features with a mix of curiosity and suspicion. The image captured a man who seemed to embody a lifetime of experiences and a certain air of enigma.

Peter Bashir, despite his advanced age of 78, displayed a spirited demeanour that suggested he refused to surrender to the passage of time. His face was etched with deep lines, each one telling a story of its own. The freckles scattered across his weathered skin spoke of youthful escapades and moments spent under the sun.

The most striking feature in the photograph was the dark circle that lurked beneath his eyes, as if shadows clung to him, hinting at the secrets he held and the darkness he had encountered throughout his life. It was a testament to the countless nights spent immersed in a world of intrigue and deception.

Bashir's eyes, while weary, retained a spark of mischief and intelligence. They held a piercing gaze that seemed to penetrate through the lens of the camera, as if he could see beyond the surface and into the depths of one's soul. It was an unsettling look, a reminder that Bashir was not to be underestimated.

His unkempt silver hair, sprinkled with hints of salt and pepper, added to the overall impression of a man who refused to conform to societal norms. There was an untamed quality to his appearance, as if he relished in the freedom of being beyond the constraints of age and convention.

The expression on Peter Bashir's face carried a certain level of unpleasantness, a hint of a cynic who had seen the darker side of humanity. It was a look that suggested he had little patience for games or pretences, and his scowl conveyed an underlying warning to those who crossed his path.

Despite his age, there was an undeniable aura of vitality surrounding him. It was as if he possessed an unyielding spirit, determined to cling onto the remnants of his youth and continue indulging in the thrill of life's adventures, albeit in a different form.

As Elizabeth held the photograph, she couldn't help but be intrigued by this complex and enigmatic figure. It suddenly struck her that moment that she still had Daniel Carter's file and had not looked into it.

Quickly, Elizabeth excused herself from her seat, feeling a sense of urgency to examine the file on Daniel Carter that she had discreetly tucked away. As she made her way to the aeroplane bathroom, she carefully navigated the narrow aisle, mindful not to draw any unnecessary attention.

Inside the compact bathroom, Elizabeth locked the door behind her and retrieved the file from her jacket pocket. With trembling hands, she opened it, eager to uncover the secrets it held. The pages contained a collection of photographs, documents, and reports meticulously gathered by intelligence agents over the years.

Elizabeth's eyes scanned the photographs, studying the face of Daniel Carter with a mix of fascination and uncertainty. The photograph revealed a middle-aged man with sharp features and an intense gaze. His German heritage was evident in his facial structure and the way he held himself.

As she examined the file further, Elizabeth discovered that Daniel Carter had indeed served as a Soviet spy at some point in his life. The details surrounding his defection remained murky, leaving unanswered questions about his motivations and subsequent actions. It was unclear where he had gone after leaving the Soviet ranks, adding another layer of mystery to his story.

The file contained a collection of photographs, each capturing Daniel Carter in various locations and situations. Some were taken in crowded city streets, others in discreet settings. It appeared as if someone had been meticulously tracking his movements, observing him from a distance.

Elizabeth couldn't help but feel a sense of unease as she studied the photographs. It seemed that Carter was being followed, his every move documented by an unknown entity. The realisation raised more questions than answers, leaving her to wonder who was behind this surveillance and why.

She carefully examined each photograph, searching for any clues or patterns that might shed light on

Carter's current whereabouts or his connection to David Scarlett. The images revealed a man who appeared both vigilant and cautious, as if constantly aware of the invisible eyes tracking his every move.

The file contained notes and observations from intelligence agents, piecing together a fragmented narrative of Carter's activities. There were references to meetings with individuals of interest, coded messages exchanged, and whispers of potential double-crosses.

Elizabeth's mind raced, trying to connect the dots and make sense of the puzzle before her. The presence of multiple photographs indicated that Carter was no ordinary individual, and the fact that he had once been a Soviet spy added another layer of complexity to his story.

As she flipped through photographs upon photographs of Daniel Carter, one particular one caught her eyes. It was Daniel Carter meeting with someone who looked so much like Peter Bashir. A little more like the younger version of Peter Bashir. While she held up the file to examine it, another picture caught her eye. This time she dropped the picture in her hands to quickly pick this one.

Elizabeth's hands trembled as she held the photograph of Daniel Carter standing next to her father. The realisation that her own father had a connection to this enigmatic figure sent a shiver down her spine. The implications were unsettling, and a rush of emotions flooded through her.

She studied the picture closely, taking in every detail. Her father stood tall and resolute, his expression serious but determined. Daniel Carter, by contrast, had a guarded look on his face, as if he carried a weighty secret. The two men seemed to share an unspoken understanding, their connection evident in the way they stood side by side.

What was her father's relationship with Daniel Carter? How did they become acquainted? And most importantly, what role did Carter play in her father's life since he was meant to be a spy and her father, a police?

This was a piece of the puzzle she couldn't ignore, a clue that demanded further investigation. And never had

Elizabeth ever felt more determined to uncover it all.

Carefully, she returned the photograph to its place in the file and secured it within her jacket once more. The urgency to find David Scarlett grew stronger within her, fueled by the haunting image of her father and the mysteries surrounding Carter's existence.

After the plane landed and Elizabeth and Emily walked out of the airport. They were greeted by the vibrant energy of Brazil. The warm tropical breeze caressed their faces as they made their way through the bustling streets. The air was filled with the lively sounds of music, chatter, and the tantalising aroma of street food.

The streets were alive with people going about their daily routines, creating a mosaic of diverse cultures and backgrounds. The streets were lined with palm trees, their swaying fronds casting shadows on the pavement. Colourful street vendors displayed their wares, offering an array of exotic fruits, handmade crafts, and traditional souvenirs.

The weather in Brazil was hot and humid, typical of its tropical climate. Beads of perspiration glistened on the brows of the people passing by, seeking relief in the shade or with a refreshing sip of coconut water sold by street vendors.

As Elizabeth and Emily navigated through the bustling streets, they couldn't help but feel the undercurrent of excitement and mystery. They were on the brink of uncovering crucial information that could lead them to David Scarlett.

Their destination, the club owned by Peter Bashir, was rumoured to be a hub of clandestine activities, where information and secrets exchanged hands under the guise of entertainment. Elizabeth's anticipation grew, fueled by the knowledge that they were getting closer to unravelling the enigma of David Scarlett.

Emily shared her strategic approach to gaining access to him. She explained that Bashir had a weakness for feminine allure and that they needed to use it to their advantage.

"We need to make a strong impression on Peter Bashir," Emily said, "He's known for being captivated by beauty and charm, so we'll play to his weaknesses."

Emily continued, "We'll wear dresses that capture his attention. Elegant, alluring outfits that reveal just enough to pique his interest but still maintain an air of sophistication."

Elizabeth listened attentively, considering the implications of their plan.

"Remember," Emily added, "Once we have his attention, we can use our skills to extract the information we need. It's about playing the game and manipulating the situation to our advantage."

'Okay.' Elizabeth nodded 'We'll need somewhere to get some clothes then.'

Emily pointed to a local clothing shop and they both walked to it. As Elizabeth and Emily entered the local clothing shop in Brazil, they were immediately greeted by a burst of vibrant colours and a lively atmosphere. The shop was a bustling hub of fashion, with rows of clothing racks and displays showcasing an array of Brazilian styles and designs.

The walls of the shop were adorned with posters and pictures of models wearing the latest trends, reflecting the vibrant culture and diversity of Brazil. The air was filled with the scent of freshly made fabrics and the sound of bustling conversation as customers and salespeople interacted with enthusiasm.

The shop was divided into sections, each offering a unique collection of clothing. Elizabeth and Emily ventured deeper into the store, their eyes captivated by the wide variety of options before them. They saw racks of flowy dresses in bold floral prints, skirts in vibrant hues, and tops adorned with intricate embroidery.

The salespeople, dressed in stylish and trendy attire themselves, moved gracefully around the shop, ready to assist Emily and Elizabeth with their fashion choices. They exude warmth and passion for their craft, eager to share their knowledge and help visitors find the perfect outfits.

The fabrics used in the clothing were of high quality, ranging from lightweight and breathable cotton for the warm Brazilian climate to luxurious silks and satins for special occasions. The textures were varied, with some garments featuring delicate ruffles, while others had playful fringes or shimmering sequins.

The shop also showcased a wide selection of accessories, from statement earrings and necklaces to colourful scarves and hats. These accessories added the finishing touches to any outfit, allowing customers to express their unique style and personality.

The fitting rooms in the shop were spacious and well-lit, providing a comfortable and private space for customers to try on their chosen garments. Mirrors adorned the walls, allowing individuals to appreciate the transformation that fashion could bring.

Throughout the shop, the sound of Portuguese filled the air as customers engaged in animated conversations with the salespeople. The vibrant energy was contagious.

Emily quickly browsed through the racks, as she carefully selected outfits that would fulfil their mission's purpose - elegant, alluring ensembles that would captivate Peter Bashir and draw him into their web of deception. She picked a particular sunset orange dress and threw it at Elizabeth.

Elizabeth hesitated for a moment, eyeing the dress that Emily had thrown at her. It was a bold, figure-hugging red dress with a plunging neckline and a slit that ran up the thigh. It was far from Elizabeth's usual style, and she couldn't help but feel a sense of discomfort.

'I'm not wearing this, Emily.' Elizabeth said, eyeing the dress in disgust.

'Yes, you are. We have 30 minutes to arrive at Peter's club. The time's ticking fast.' Emily said and quickly left for a changing room.

Lifted the dress up again in disgust and walked into the changing room to try it on. Inside the changing room, Elizabeth examined the dress in more detail. The fabric was smooth and luxurious, clinging to her skin as she held it up against her body. The vibrant orange colour seemed to demand attention, and she couldn't deny the allure it exuded.

With a sigh, Elizabeth began to undress, carefully slipping out of her previous attire. As she put on the bright orange dress, she couldn't help but notice how it accentuated her curves. However, she struggled with the dress.

She fumbled with the zipper, desperately trying to free herself from its tight embrace, which made her frustration grow. But amidst her attempts, she couldn't help but catch snippets of a conversation taking place on the other side of the shop.

Curiosity sparked within her, and she leaned closer, straining to hear the hushed voices. The shopkeeper and another person seemed to be engaged in a quiet discussion, their words muffled but gradually becoming clearer.

"...unusual activity...recently...heard rumours...dangerous...be careful..."

The words floated in the air, incomplete but enough to pique Elizabeth's interest. Her initial annoyance at the dress was momentarily forgotten as she focused on deciphering the conversation. She silently eased herself closer, careful not to attract any attention.

"...undoubtedly connected...the past...secrets...keep an eye..."

Elizabeth's heart raced as she strained to catch every word. The fragments of conversation hinted at something significant, something potentially related to their mission. She couldn't afford to miss any details.

"...Peter Bashir...agreement...involved...Russian spy..."

As Elizabeth listened intently, the conversation continued to unfold, revealing more about the upcoming events at Peter Bashir's club. The shopkeeper's voice grew clearer, emphasising the significance of the night ahead.

"...carnival...tonight...Peter Bashir's grand spectacle...all his ladies on display..."

Elizabeth's eyebrows furrowed as she tried to make sense of the conversation. The mention of a carnival sparked her curiosity. It seemed that Peter Bashir had something extravagant planned, a spectacle designed to captivate and enthral the crowd.

The other voice chimed in, sharing additional details.

"...unforgettable...the ladies...they'll blow the crowd away...dazzling costumes, mesmerising performances..."

Elizabeth's mind raced with possibilities. The carnival appeared to be an event where Peter Bashir showcased his ladies, possibly dancers or performers, in a grand and spectacular fashion. The mention of dazzling costumes and mesmerising performances hinted at a night filled with visual splendour and intrigue.

Realising the potential significance of attending the carnival, Elizabeth felt a surge of determination. It could provide an opportunity to gain insight into Peter Bashir's world and potentially uncover information about David Scarlett.

A mosquito perched on Elizabeth's shoulders. Startled, she tried as quickly as she could to whisk it off without making a sound. Thankfully she killed it before it got away. Realising she had been distracted from the conversation, Elizabeth leaned in to hear more

'...exactly...David
Scarlett...hiding...tonight.'

Elizabeth's heart skipped a beat as the name "David Scarlett" resurfaced in the conversation. It was a jolt that snapped her back to attention, her mind instantly focused on the significance of those words.

Struggling to make sense of the connection, Elizabeth tried to piece together the fragments she had overheard. How had David Scarlett's name entered the conversation? Was he somehow linked to Peter Bashir or the carnival? The questions swirled in her mind, demanding answers.

She wished she had been more attentive, as her momentary distraction had caused her to miss crucial details. However, one thing was clear: David Scarlett's presence in the conversation indicated that he held a significant role in the web of secrets surrounding Peter Bashir and his activities.

Elizabeth strained her ears and listened attentively to the conversation between the two strangers at the other side of the changing room...

'I heard he's expecting someone special to join him tonight...'

'...about this David Scarlett character. He said he's quite notorious...'

Elizabeth's heart leapt. David Scarlett was coming in tonight!

Elizabeth couldn't contain her excitement as she relayed the information she had overheard to Emily. Emily's expression changed, realising the significance of this new development.

'So, David Scarlett is expected to be at Peter Bashir's carnival tonight? That changes everything. We can use this to our advantage.'

'We can plan an ambush tonight', Elizabeth said

Emily nodded in agreement, and they quickly hailed a cab to Peter Bashir's club. The anticipation was building, and they couldn't help but feel a sense of urgency. They arrived at the club, the vibrant sounds of music and laughter filling the air.

As Emily and Elizabeth entered Peter Bashir's club, they were immediately engulfed in a vibrant and energetic atmosphere. The club was alive with the rhythmic beats of Brazilian music, creating an irresistible urge to move to the infectious tunes. The air was thick with anticipation and excitement, as people swayed their hips and danced to the pulsating rhythms.

The scent of exotic cocktails and traditional Brazilian cuisine wafted through the air, tempting the taste buds of the clubgoers. The bar was a hub of activity, with skilled bartenders expertly crafting colourful and enticing drinks. The sound of clinking glasses and laughter filled the air, creating an atmosphere of joy and celebration.

The energy on the dance floor was infectious. Couples twirled and spun in perfect harmony, showcasing their impressive dance skills. The infectious rhythms of samba, bossa nova, and other Brazilian genres pulsed through the club, compelling everyone to join in the celebration.

In the midst of the lively crowd, Emily and Elizabeth navigated their way towards Peter Bashir, their eyes scanning the room for any signs of the man who held the key to unlocking the secrets they sought. The vibrant and electrifying ambience of the club served as the backdrop for their mission, as they prepared to approach Bashir.

Emily approached a bodyguard and whispered some things in his ears. He nodded and walked them to a quiet room which had a giant neon-lit label Bashir's Private Club.

As Emily and Elizabeth made their entrance into Peter Bashir's club, their transformed appearance caught the attention of everyone in the room. The click of their high silhouette heels echoed through the space, commanding attention with every step. Their confident stride and captivating presence turned heads as they made their way towards the upper part of the club where Peter Bashir was...

Emily's once-restrained hair was now styled in loose waves that cascaded down her shoulders, adding a touch of glamour to her look. Her eyes were accentuated with smokey eyeshadow, and her lips were painted a bold shade of red, exuding a sense of allure and sophistication.

Elizabeth, on the other hand, had opted for a more daring hairstyle, her usually wavy short strands were graced with long full wavy extensions with strands of wavy fringe, giving her an exotic look. Her eyes were adorned with dramatic eyeliner, emphasising their intensity, while her lips sported a deep, seductive shade that matched the air of mystery surrounding her.

Their choice of heavy makeup enhanced their features, adding an air of mystery and intrigue. The carefully applied foundation created a flawless canvas, while the expertly contoured cheekbones highlighted their bone structure. Their eyes, accentuated with dark eyelashes and perfectly blended eyeshadow, exuded a sense of confidence and determination.

Their attire reflected a newfound sense of femininity and sensuality. Elizabeth wore a form-fitting orange dress that hugged her curves, accentuating her figure, while Emily opted for a vibrant red dress that flowed gracefully with her movements, commanding attention from all who laid eyes on her.

As they walked further into the club, the combination of their transformed appearances and the infectious energy of the crowd drew curious glances from onlookers. They knew that their new appearances would catch the attention of Peter Bashir and create a lasting impression, ensuring they slate their way through the mission successfully...

As Emily and Elizabeth were escorted by the bodyguard through the crowd, Elizabeth couldn't help but observe Emily's captivating transformation. It was as if Emily had stepped into a different persona, effortlessly embodying a newfound femininity and grace that complemented her every move.

Emily's posture exuded confidence and allure, her body swaying with a subtle rhythm that commanded attention. Her steps were deliberate and graceful, as if she were gliding through the crowd, effortlessly navigating the sea of bodies with poise and elegance. Elizabeth noticed how Emily's shoulders relaxed, her back straightened, and her hips subtly swayed, accentuating her feminine curves.

It wasn't just Emily's physical transformation that struck Elizabeth; it was the way she carried herself, the way she commanded attention while putting aside her arrogant or overpowering attitude. There was a certain magnetism about her that made it clear she was in control of the situation, effortlessly manipulating her femininity to her advantage.

Elizabeth couldn't help but feel a mix of admiration and intrigue. She had always known Emily to be a skilled agent, but witnessing her seamless transition into this new persona left her in awe. It was as if Emily had unlocked a hidden part of herself, tapping into a wellspring of feminine power that she wielded with precision and finesse.

They soon got to where Peter Bashir was and were asked to stand in line where the bodyguard walked up to him and whispered a few things in his ears.

Peter Bashir's imposing figure sat before them, larger and more intimidating than he appeared in the picture. His broad shoulders and muscular frame emanating strength and power. The cigar clutched between his fingers emitted a faint trail of smoke, swirling around him like a veil of mystery.

His cold, piercing eyes bore into them, seemingly assessing them and scrutinising their presence. The lines on his face spoke of a lifetime of experiences, etched with a hint of weariness and a hardened edge. His expression was guarded, revealing little of his true intentions or emotions.

Elizabeth couldn't help but feel a shiver run down her spine as she met his gaze. The intensity of his stare sent a chill through her, like being caught in the crosshairs of a predator. His presence commanded respect, and his aura exuded an air of danger.

Soon a flicker of recognition and appreciation danced across his face, as the bodyguard continued the whispers in his ears. His once cold and menacing expression transformed into one of delight and intrigue. It was as if he had been captivated by the sheer beauty and allure of the two women before him.

With a subtle wave of his hand, Peter Bashir motioned to his bodyguards to have them step forward. His eyes locked onto Elizabeth again, his gaze filled with a mixture of interest and curiosity. Elizabeth couldn't help but feel a tinge of unease, uncertain of what Peter Bashir's intentions were or what he had said to his guards.

The bodyguards, following their employer's orders, shifted their attention towards Elizabeth. Their eyes were filled with a combination of vigilance and scrutiny as they carefully observed her every move.

Elizabeth's heart skipped a beat as the bodyguard delivered the unexpected message. She glanced over at Emily, who raised an eyebrow in surprise. It seemed that Peter Bashir had taken a particular interest in Elizabeth and had chosen her to be his escort for the festival.

Caught off guard by the sudden turn of events, Elizabeth quickly composed herself and nodded in acknowledgement to the bodyguard. She couldn't help but feel a mixture of apprehension and curiosity about what this role entailed and what Peter Bashir's intentions might be.

As the bodyguard escorted her closer to Peter Bashir, Elizabeth's mind raced. Approaching Peter Bashir, Elizabeth was met with an intense gaze that seemed to dissect her every move. His eyes held a hint of amusement and satisfaction, as if he relished the anticipation of the upcoming festival and the company of his chosen escort.

Elizabeth noticed that Peter Bashir seemed to revel in the attention he received with her by his side. His demeanour shifted from menacing to jovial, as if the presence of a beautiful woman had momentarily lifted the weight of his darker side

Peter Bashir's words hung in the air, and Elizabeth strained to listen as he addressed Emily. The surrounding noise seemed to fade away as she focused on their conversation.

"Miss Jenny," Peter Bashir said, addressing Emily, his tone laced with a mix of anticipation and authority. "I have a special request for you tonight. I heard you're one of the greatest belly dancers out here. I would be delighted if you would grace us with a private dance, exclusively for me and my esteemed guests."

Emily maintained her composed demeanour, her expression giving away nothing. "Of course, Mr Bashir," she replied, her voice laced with a hint of intrigue. "I would be honoured to perform for you and your guests."

Peter Bashir's eyes glimmered with satisfaction. "Excellent," he said, a smug grin playing on his lips. "I have prepared a secluded area where you can showcase your talents. It will be an intimate affair, and I expect nothing less than perfection from you."

Elizabeth watched as Emily nodded, accepting the challenge laid before her. As Peter Bashir and Emily continued their conversation, discussing the logistics of the private dance, Elizabeth couldn't help but marvel at Emily's ability to seamlessly slip into various roles. Emily's determination to do whatever it took to get closer to their target was both impressive and unsettling.

It was at that moment she finally understood the true meaning behind Emily's self-proclaimed identity as a "slithering green snake." Emily had spent years honing her abilities and establishing multiple trusted identities in different locations, earning the trust of those around her through careful observation, cunning, and adaptability.

In London, Emily had mastered the art of blending into the background, becoming a mysterious lady who seemingly faded into the shadows but had her keen eyes fixated on every detail. She possessed a sharp intellect and a knack for analysing situations, making her a valuable asset in gathering information and deciphering complex webs of intrigue.

In Germany, Emily had seamlessly integrated herself into the local community, adopting the customs, language, and mannerisms of the people. She possessed a charm that allowed her to politely request access to places that others would be denied, even gaining entry into the mansion of a notorious espionage lord. Her ability to effortlessly navigate different social circles and blend in with the locals spoke volumes about her adaptability and resourcefulness.

And now, in Brazil, Emily had established a reputation as a mesmerising belly dancer. It was yet another facet of her multifaceted identity, enabling her to move in circles that might otherwise be closed off to outsiders. Emily knew how to use her allure and femininity to captivate others, gaining access to information and earning the trust of those who held valuable secrets.

Despite Emily's occasional arrogance, Elizabeth couldn't deny the fact that she knew what she was doing. Emily had proven time and again that she was not just a mere agent but a force to be reckoned with. Her arrogance was not misplaced, but rather a reflection of her unwavering confidence in her abilities and her track record of success.

The plan was clear to Elizabeth now. She would position herself by Peter Bashir's side, acting as his escort for the evening. From this vantage point, she would have the opportunity to closely observe the interactions between Peter Bashir and his guests, keeping a keen ear out for any mention of David Scarlett. Her sharp instincts would guide her in detecting any suspicious behaviour or conversations that could lead them closer to their target.

Meanwhile, Emily would take centre stage with her captivating belly dance performance. As the guests' attention would be captivated by Emily's mesmerising movements, Elizabeth would seize the opportunity to discreetly slip away, blending into the shadows of the club. Her mission was clear: search for any trace of David Scarlett, be it documents, photographs, or any form of evidence that could shed light on his activities.

As the evening progressed, Elizabeth focused her attention on Peter Bashir, maintaining a poised demeanour while her eyes and ears remained ever vigilant. She tuned in to every conversation, every subtle exchange of words, hoping to catch a hint of David Scarlett's presence or plans.

Emily, clad in her vibrant costume, took to the dance floor with grace and precision. Her movements were spellbinding, capturing the attention of everyone in the room. Elizabeth marvelled at her partner's ability to command the stage, knowing that her distraction was essential for their plan to succeed.

Stealthily, Elizabeth slipped away from Peter Bashir's side, slipping into the depths of the club's interior. She moved with purpose, her senses heightened, searching every corner for any signs of David Scarlett's involvement. She rifled through files, scanned photographs, and meticulously examined any documents that might hold clues.

Time seemed to both stretch and blur as Elizabeth delved deeper into the club's hidden spaces. Every creak of the floorboards, every distant murmur of conversation heightened her senses. She was on the brink of discovery when she felt a tap behind her.

'What are doing here' someone said in Portuguese

Elizabeth's heart sank as she was intercepted by a sharp-eyed guard, his grip firm on her arm. She cursed herself for the momentary lapse in her stealth, realising that her intrusion had been detected. The guard led her back towards the main area of the club, where Peter Bashir and the guests watched Emily's performance.

As they approached the dance floor, Elizabeth's mind raced, searching for a way to salvage the situation. She knew that her capture could jeopardise their mission to uncover David Scarlett's whereabouts. She needed to act swiftly and decisively.

Feigning a sense of panic, Elizabeth stumbled forward, tripping over her own feet as she purposely caught the attention of Peter Bashir and the crowd. Her actions drew gasps and concerned murmurs from the onlookers. Emily, quick on her feet, seized the opportunity to improvise, incorporating Elizabeth's supposed mishap into her dance routine.

With every graceful movement, Emily diverted the attention away from Elizabeth's capture. The crowd was captivated by her performance, their gaze fixed on her mesmerising presence.

She moved with fluidity and grace, her body swaying to the rhythm of the music that enveloped the room. As the enticing melody filled the air, her movements synchronised perfectly, captivating the audience with each subtle sway and deliberate step.

Her hips undulated sensually, each movement executed with precision and confidence. The sheer fluidity of her motions seemed to defy the laws of gravity, as if she were floating on air. The glimmering lights of the club reflected off her shimmering costume, casting an ethereal glow around her.

Emily's arms glided through the air, their graceful arcs and intricate patterns adding to the allure of her performance. Every extension of her limbs was purposeful, accentuating the rhythm of the music and drawing the eyes of the mesmerised onlookers.

With each beat, Emily's body seemed to come alive, expressing emotions and desires through her undulating torso. Her torso rolled and twisted, creating a hypnotic display of sensuality and control. The subtlest of gestures conveyed a story, enticing the audience to delve deeper into the depths of her artistry.

As the tempo of the music intensified, Emily's movements became more energetic, captivating the crowd with her sheer passion and raw talent. She seamlessly transitioned between fluid and sharp movements, showcasing her versatility as a dancer.

The intensity in her eyes was palpable, radiating an alluring mix of confidence and vulnerability. Her gaze swept across the room, locking eyes with individuals in the audience, drawing them into her world of seduction and mystery. It was as if she held a secret that could only be discovered through the language of her body.

The rhythm of the drums quickened, echoing the pounding of hearts in the room. Emily's footwork became faster, her feet tapping and gliding across the dance floor with precision and control. Each step exuded power and determination, reinforcing the magnetism of her performance.

The audience was enthralled, their gaze fixated on every movement, every expression that flickered across Emily's face.

The atmosphere in the club shifted as the group of menacing men in black entered the room, their presence immediately commanding attention. Elizabeth's heart skipped a beat as she recognized them as the same individuals responsible for the death of Crane. The air grew heavy with tension, and a sense of impending danger hung in the air.

Peter Bashir's face contorted into a mixture of surprise and apprehension as the men approached him with an air of authority. Their cold, calculated expressions sent a shiver down Elizabeth's spine, and she knew that this encounter would not bode well for anyone involved.

The crowd fell into an uneasy silence as the men exchanged hushed words with Bashir. Elizabeth strained to catch snippets of their conversation, her instincts urging her to uncover any clue about their intentions. She could sense the imminent danger that lurked within their presence, the weight of unfinished business

Immediately Bashir stood up and waved to his bodyguards, who followed him immediately down the hall. Elizabeth followed Peter Bashir stealthily, careful not to make a sound as she trailed him and his bodyguards through a labyrinth of corridors and rooms. Her heart raced with anticipation, the gravity of the situation fueling her determination to uncover the truth.

As she continued to shadow Bashir, Elizabeth's senses sharpened, her ears attuned to the faintest of sounds. She observed his movements, noting the way he glanced over his shoulder every now and then, a sign of his awareness that he might be followed.

Finally, Peter Bashir reached a secluded room tucked away at the end of a dimly lit hallway with his bodyguards firmly guarding the door.

Elizabeth managed to find a hidden passage adjacent to the room where Peter Bashir and the mysterious person had gathered. The narrow passage provided her with a vantage point, allowing her to eavesdrop on their conversation without being detected.

She held her breath, her heart pounding in her chest, as the voices within the room grew clearer. Every word spoken held vital information that could potentially unravel the web of intrigue surrounding David Scarlett and his connection to Peter Bashir.

From her concealed position, Elizabeth strained her ears to catch every fragment of the conversation. Their voices were hushed, laden with intensity and secrecy. The exchange was cryptic, filled with coded language and veiled references that hinted at a larger conspiracy.

Peter Bashir's voice, tinged with a mix of nervousness and determination, revealed that he was deeply involved in an operation with significant implications. He spoke of a "package" that had arrived and the urgency of the situation.

The other mysterious person in the room responded with calculated precision, his voice cold and commanding. Her heart skipped a beat as the conversation shifted to a Russian spy with a secret code capable of infiltrating nuclear facilities in seven key countries of the West. The gravity of the situation intensified, and Elizabeth's mind raced to comprehend the enormity of the threat posed by this covert operation.

The details surrounding the Russian spy and their code were vague, but the urgency in Peter Bashir's voice was unmistakable. He spoke of the spy's importance in the operation and the need to protect the code at all costs.

Elizabeth's mind raced with the implications of this new information. The involvement of a Russian spy added another layer of complexity to the already intricate web of espionage and international intrigue. She knew that exposing this spy's identity and disrupting their plans was crucial to preventing a potential disaster.

As the conversation continued, Elizabeth strained to catch any additional details that could aid her mission. She noted that the spy's codename was mentioned.

Elizabeth's mind was overwhelmed with a flurry of thoughts and questions. How did David Scarlett fit into this intricate puzzle? Was he working in tandem with the Russian spy, or were their operations separate yet intertwined? The missing pieces of the puzzle eluded her, creating a frustrating sense of confusion and urgency.

As Elizabeth continued to eavesdrop on the conversation between Peter Bashir and the mysterious personality in the room, a shocking realisation struck her like a lightning bolt. Contrary to her previous assumptions, it became clear that Peter Bashir and this individual were not collaborating with David Scarlett. Instead, they viewed him as a formidable threat to their own operation and were determined to neutralise him.

Elizabeth's heart pounded in her chest as she absorbed the gravity of this revelation. The intricate web of alliances and counteralliances became even more convoluted. It seemed that everyone involved in this tangled web of espionage had their own motives and agendas, with David Scarlett standing at the centre as a dangerous wild card.

The Russian spy agent, whose existence is now a source of concern, was now revealed to be a key player in the plot against David Scarlett.

It was evident that Peter Bashir and his companion saw David Scarlett as a significant threat, one who could potentially expose their operation and compromise their objectives. Their goal was to eliminate him before he could pose any further danger to their plans. Elizabeth realised that their interests aligned with her own, at least in the short term.

Elizabeth's mind whirled with a cascade of questions. If the Russian spy agent was as formidable as David Scarlett, why had the intelligence agencies focused their efforts solely on capturing David Scarlett? Why was the Russian spy seemingly untouchable, operating freely while carrying out his nefarious activities?

As she pondered these puzzling dynamics, Elizabeth considered the possibility of a larger game at play. It appeared that the intelligence agencies were aware of the Russian spy's existence and his connection to the plot targeting key nuclear facilities. Yet, their focus remained fixed on David Scarlett, leaving the Russian spy's operations largely unchecked.

She contemplated the possibility that the intelligence agencies were playing a dangerous game of manipulation and misdirection. Perhaps they saw David Scarlett as a more immediate and tangible target, while the Russian spy operated with a veil of secrecy and protection. It was also possible that the Russian spy had powerful connections or information that made him a challenging target for conventional law enforcement.

Deep in thought, Elizabeth considered the potential consequences of exposing the Russian spy. Bringing down someone of his calibre would require extensive resources and cooperation from multiple intelligence agencies. It was a daunting task.

However, the Russian spy's ability to infiltrate nuclear facilities in key countries posed a severe threat to global security. The potential devastation that could result from his actions sent chills down her spine. It was no longer just about capturing David Scarlett; it was about dismantling an entire network and preventing an imminent disaster. She could not be quiet about this.

Elizabeth heard a faint sound of a siren. It felt quite distant at first till the whole building was consumed by the sound of the siren and the blue and red flashes of light. Within a blink of an eye, Elizabeth realised the entire building had been surrounded by the S.I.S (Secret Intelligence Service) force, armed to the teeth and ready for action. It became apparent that Emily had called for backup, hoping that David Scarlett was present and that this would be their opportunity to apprehend him.

The sudden arrival of the S.I.S agents sent waves of chaos and panic throughout the building. Doors were forced open, and the agents flooded in, their presence commanding authority. The sound of heavy footsteps echoed through the halls as they swiftly moved from room to room, searching for their targets.

Elizabeth found herself caught up in the frenzy, as agents pushed past her, their expressions determined and focused. Their eyes scanned the surroundings, their fingers firmly on the triggers of their weapons. The tension in the air was palpable as they meticulously ransacked the premises in their quest for David Scarlett.

Amidst the chaos, Elizabeth's mind raced to comprehend the rapidly unfolding situation. The hope of capturing David Scarlett and preventing further harm seemed within reach. However, she couldn't help but feel a sense of disappointment that the Russian spy agents had managed to escape. The helicopter's whirr in the distance signalled their successful evasion.

As the agents moved systematically through the building, Elizabeth caught glimpses of Peter Bashir being apprehended. His face registered a mix of shock and resignation, knowing that his schemes had come to an abrupt end. She wondered what information he might possess and if it would shed light on the larger conspiracy involving the Russian spy and their network.

The scene resembled a carefully choreographed dance of authority and efficiency. The agents, with their unwavering determination, methodically swept through each room, ensuring that no stone was left unturned. Cabinets were opened, furniture overturned, and any potential hiding places thoroughly searched.

As the S.I.S forces surrounded Peter Bashir, a hushed silence fell over the room. Elizabeth watched with bated breath as Emily calmly approached, her gaze fixed on Peter's face. There was an unmistakable air of authority and confidence emanating from her, revealing a side of Emily that Peter had never seen before.

A flicker of recognition crossed Peter's face as he locked eyes with Emily. It was a look of horror mixed with disbelief, as if a puzzle piece he thought he had solved had suddenly transformed into a complex enigma.

Emily's expression remained unreadable as she stood before Peter, her posture commanding and her voice filled with authority. At that moment, the truth became undeniable: Emily was not who she appeared to be. She had been an agent all along, skillfully concealing her true identity while operating under the guise of a trusted confidante.

While the S.I.S forces maintained a tight grip on Peter, their steely gazes reflecting their readiness to swiftly respond to any resistance, Peter pleaded his innocence, desperately proclaiming his lack of involvement with David Scarlett. Yet, the S.I.S agents remained resolute in their duty. They regarded Peter with a steely resolve, their expressions unmoved by his protestations. With a firm grip on his arms, they led him away from the room, disappearing into the depths of the building.

Elizabeth watched as Peter was taken away, she couldn't help but question the veracity of his claims.
'Emily,' Elizabeth walked up to Emily 'I overheard their conversation. It wasn't about David Scarlett. Peter Bashir was actually plotting against him. He and this Russian spy were in an alliance, planning to bring down David Scarlett and his mission. The men with them were not working for David Scarlett but for this mysterious Russian guy. We need to consider the bigger picture here.

Emily looked at Elizabeth confused 'Our primary objective is David Scarlett. That's what we've been tasked with, and that's where our focus needs to be. Any other players or alliances are secondary to our mission.'

'Yes, but this Russian spy has the ability to infiltrate nuclear facilities in key countries. He poses a more significant threat to global security. We can't just ignore it.'

'Look, Elizabeth, I understand your concerns, but we are not in a position to make those decisions. Our job is to follow orders and capture David Scarlett. '

Elizabeth persisted, 'But what if there's a connection between David Scarlett and the Russian spy? What if their operations are intertwined? We could be missing a crucial piece of the puzzle.'

'Elizabeth! We don't have the authority or the resources to investigate this further. Our job is to provide actionable intelligence regarding David Scarlett's activities.' Emily said firmly and walked away.

CHAPTER SEVEN: SHADOWS OF THE PAST

Elizabeth walked the streets of London, her thoughts consumed by the events in Brazil and the lingering questions that plagued her. The bustling cityscape provided little solace as she pondered the possible implications of their mission. It was clear that something larger was at play, and the Russian spy's involvement had raised significant concerns.

The weather shifted abruptly as dark clouds loomed overhead, casting a shadow over the once-bright London streets. The first droplets of rain began to fall, gently at first, but gradually gaining intensity. Elizabeth, caught off guard by the sudden change, hurriedly reached into her bag and pulled out a trusty umbrella.

As she opened it, the canopy unfurled like a shield against the relentless downpour. The rhythmic sound of raindrops hitting the pavement enveloped her as she continued her walk, determined to find solace in the midst of the storm. The city seemed to transform, taking on a different aura in the rain. The vibrant colours of the buildings turned muted, and the hurried footsteps of passersby echoed through the emptying streets.

With each step, the rhythmic pitter-patter of rain against the umbrella became a meditative soundtrack, temporarily drowning out the whirlwind of thoughts and uncertainties that had plagued her mind. The world seemed to slow down, allowing her to focus on the present moment.

Elizabeth's mind wandered back to the events that unfolded after Peter Bashir's arrest. Despite his denial of any involvement with David Scarlett or the Russian spy agency, there was something about Peter's demeanour that sparked her curiosity. He seemed genuinely against David Scarlett, just like Elizabeth and Emily were, and he appeared willing to provide them with valuable information.

Elizabeth mulled over the possibilities. Could Peter be a reluctant ally, someone caught between the machinations of powerful players? Or was there a deeper layer of deception at play? The ambiguity of the situation only heightened her determination to uncover the truth.

She recalled the conversation she overheard between Peter and the mysterious personality in the room. The mention of the Russian spy and his plans to infiltrate nuclear facilities in key countries sent a chill down her spine. The stakes were higher than she had initially realized. If David Scarlett's mission was to thwart the Russian spy, then perhaps their objectives aligned more closely than she had assumed.

Elizabeth's thoughts raced as she considered the implications of Peter's accounts. It didn't align with the information she had gathered from eavesdropping on his conversation. The discrepancy raised red flags and shattered any trust she had momentarily placed in Peter's words.

If Peter was intentionally providing false information, it meant that he was not only deceitful but also potentially dangerous. Elizabeth couldn't shake the feeling that working closely with someone who was willing to manipulate the truth could compromise the integrity of their mission and the safety of the S.I.S. team.

The rain continued to pour, mirroring Elizabeth's growing unease. She knew that she couldn't afford to be swayed by false narratives or misplaced trust. It was crucial to remain objective, follow the evidence, and make informed decisions.

Elizabeth had realized that she needed to approach her superiors in the S.I.S. She had a responsibility to report her findings and voice her concerns. It was essential to ensure that all relevant information was taken into account and that the team's actions were based on the most accurate and reliable intelligence available.

However, her superiors dismissed her claims as irrelevant. The weight of frustration and helplessness bore down on her shoulders. It was disheartening to see that her concerns were not taken seriously, especially when the safety of the S.I.S. and the potential threat of the Russian spy hung in the balance.

In the midst of the pouring rain, Elizabeth felt a sense of isolation. She was acutely aware that she stood alone in her convictions, with no support from those who held the power to enact change. It was as if her voice was lost in the cacophony of raindrops pelting the ground around her.

However, Elizabeth refused to let this setback deter her. The mission's significance loomed larger than ever, and the truth needed to be uncovered. With renewed determination, she resolved to continue her pursuit of David Scarlett and the Russian spy, even if it meant going against the wishes of her superiors.

As she walked through the rain-soaked streets, Elizabeth realized that she couldn't rely solely on the established hierarchy. She needed to find allies within the S.I.S who shared her concerns, individuals who recognized the importance of the bigger picture and were willing to challenge the prevailing narrative.

Elizabeth stepped out of the cold, wet streets and into the warmth of her apartment, shaking off the droplets of rain from her umbrella. The sound of rain still echoed in her ears as she closed the door behind her, grateful for the sanctuary of her cosy abode.

She leaned her umbrella against the wall and took a deep breath, revelling in the comforting familiarity of her home. The soft glow of the lamps illuminated the living room, casting a gentle, calming ambiance. The scent of home filled the air, creating a sense of peace and solace.

Seeking respite from the chill outside, Elizabeth made her way to the kitchen. She filled the kettle with fresh water and set it on the stove, the flame dancing beneath it. As she waited for the water to boil, she reached for her favourite blend of tea, carefully selecting the leaves that would soon steep in the warm water.

With a cup in hand, Elizabeth settled into a plush armchair, wrapping herself in a cosy blanket. The rhythmic sound of the rain on the windows provided a soothing background melody, lulling her into a state of tranquillity. She took a moment to savour the fragrance of the tea leaves, the steam rising and caressing her face.

Just as she settled into the peace of the moment, she heard a faint knock on the door, interrupting the serenity of her solitude. Curiosity piqued, Elizabeth set her tea down and made her way to the door, wondering who could be seeking her company on such a rainy evening.

Elizabeth opened the door to find Hugh standing there, raindrops cascading down his tall frame. His usually impeccable appearance was slightly dishevelled, with rain-soaked hair clinging to his forehead and his clothes glistening from the downpour. Despite the dampness, his piercing blue eyes sparkled with a mix of determination and concern.

A small smile played at the corners of Hugh's lips, but it was overshadowed by a seriousness in his expression. His strong jawline and chiselled features were accentuated by the wetness on his face, giving him a rugged and enigmatic air. It was as if the rain had only enhanced his charismatic presence.

Dressed in a black shirt that clung to his broad shoulders, Hugh exuded an air of confidence despite the rain-soaked surroundings. He stood with a certain poise.

As Elizabeth's gaze travelled down, she noticed the raindrops gliding down his firm chest. The rain continued to fall, casting a misty backdrop that added an ethereal quality to the moment. Elizabeth couldn't help but feel a sense of intrigue and curiosity as she locked eyes with Hugh.

'Come in.' she finally said and invited him in.

The room fell into a momentary silence as Elizabeth and Hugh settled into their seats, raindrops tapping against the windowpane in a soothing rhythm. It was as if the weight of their past disagreements hung in the air, begging to be acknowledged.

Breaking the silence, Hugh cleared his throat and spoke with sincerity in his voice. "I wanted to apologize for our past differences. The circumstances were difficult, and I allowed my emotions to cloud my judgment. I regret any hurt I may have caused."

Elizabeth's eyes met Hugh's, and she could see genuine remorse reflected in his gaze. Taking a deep breath, she nodded in understanding. "Hugh, I also owe you an apology. I let my stubbornness get in the way, and I didn't fully consider your perspective. I shouldn't have put it in such a position."

Taking a deep breath, Elizabeth began to share her recent discoveries. She recounted her encounter with Peter Bashir, his arrest, and the subsequent realization that he was not working with David Scarlett, but rather with a dangerous Russian spy. With each word, she conveyed her growing unease and her concerns about the misinformation and the potential threat to national security.

Hugh listened attentively, his brows furrowing as Elizabeth unfolded the intricacies of the situation. He could sense the weight of her words, the gravity of her findings.

When Elizabeth finished recounting her discoveries, she looked at Hugh, searching his eyes for a glimmer of recognition. "Hugh," she began, her voice filled with anticipation, "have you ever heard anything about this Russian spy guy?"

Hugh leaned back, his expression contemplative. "Elizabeth," he said slowly, "I can't say that I have direct knowledge of this particular situation. But the intelligence community is vast, and information can sometimes be compartmentalized. It's possible that certain pieces of the puzzle have eluded me."

"I see," she replied, a tinge of disappointment evident in her voice.

Hugh reached out and placed a comforting hand on hers. "Elizabeth, I assure you that you will be the first to know I know anything about this guy.'

They sat in silence for a moment, the sound of rain providing a gentle backdrop to their thoughts. Elizabeth finally broke the silence, her voice filled with determination. "Hugh, I can't rest until I've uncovered this truth. I mean, everything feels so distant and all over the place but I can't help but tell just a pull of a string could tie everything all up...'

As Elizabeth continued to speak, frustration began to colour her words. She expressed her disappointment in the lack of progress, the dismissive attitude of her superiors, and the feeling that her findings were falling on deaf ears. Each detail she shared carried a sense of urgency, a plea for someone to take her concerns seriously.

She told Hugh of the danger posed by the Russian spy and his plans to undermine the West, highlighting the potentially catastrophic consequences if action was not taken swiftly. With each passing moment, Elizabeth's frustration grew, fueled by the knowledge that time was slipping away and the threat loomed larger with every passing day.

She spoke with fervour as she was passionate about her mission and was deeply committed to protecting her country. Yet, the lack of support and validation she received from her superiors only added to her mounting frustration.

Elizabeth questioned the motives behind their reluctance to acknowledge the Russian spy's involvement. She couldn't understand why they were fixated on David Scarlett, who seemed to be a mere pawn in a much larger game. It felt as though the truth was being obscured, deliberately or unintentionally, and she couldn't help but feel a growing sense of disillusionment.

She explained how Peter had implicated David Scarlett as the mastermind behind the plans to infiltrate the West with a secret code. However, Elizabeth had overheard a conversation between Peter and the Russian spy, where it was clear that the real threat came from the Russian agent himself.

In her frustration, Elizabeth pondered the significance of her role within the intelligence community. She wondered if her voice truly mattered, if her findings would ever be given the attention they deserved.

As Elizabeth poured out her frustrations, Hugh listened attentively, his expression a mix of empathy and concern. He understood the weight she carried and the toll it was taking on her. He offered words of encouragement, assuring her that her perseverance and dedication would eventually lead to the truth being revealed.

'...maybe things would have made a little bit of sense when we went to Reinhardt's mansion and I saw this Daniel Carter's file who has ties to my dad and many of these bad guys.'

As Elizabeth mentioned Daniel Carter, a flicker of recognition crossed Hugh's face. He leaned forward, his curiosity piqued,

'Daniel Carter? What do you mean...wait, backtrack a bit. How did you find out about Daniel Carter?'

Elizabeth, eager to share her findings, provided a detailed account of the visit to Reinhardt's mansion and the connections she had uncovered between Peter Bashir, the Russian spy, and Daniel Carter. In her investigation, she had discovered that Daniel Carter was a highly skilled intelligence operative, known for his expertise in counterintelligence and covert operations.

Hugh's expression turned thoughtful as he listened to Elizabeth's account.

'Do you know anything about him?' Elizabeth's expression softened as she decided to hear from Hugh.

'Daniel Carter? Yes, I'm familiar with him. He's an exceptional intelligence operative known for his expertise in counterintelligence and covert operations. But what connections have you discovered between him and the Russian spy?'

'I don't know Hugh. I find him to be a very strange man.' Elizabeth got up and excused herself. She came back with the picture of Daniel Carter and her father she found in Reinhardt's mansion. 'Look,' she gave the picture to Hugh, 'how could such a man who is linked to high espionage networks be associated with my dad.

Hugh sat back, he gazed at the picture thoughtfully "Elizabeth," he began, "Daniel Carter was not just any intelligence operative. He was a close friend of your father's."

"My father?" Elizabeth's eyes widened in surprise. "I never knew he had connections in the world of espionage."

'No, your father was not involved in covert operations. It was Daniel who was before he decided to leave that world behind and join the police force. He and Daniel were partners, working together on numerous high-stakes missions. He had no idea at the beginning of their partnership what Daniel had been involved in"

Hugh continued, "Daniel Carter was renowned for his exceptional skills and unwavering dedication to the mission. He and your father formed an inseparable team, relying on each other's instincts and expertise to overcome the challenges they faced."

Elizabeth leaned forward, her curiosity piqued. "Tell me more about Daniel," she urged, wanting to uncover every detail of her father's past and his connection to this mysterious figure.

Hugh obliged, painting a vivid picture of Daniel's character. He described him as someone with an unwavering moral compass, a man of integrity who would stop at nothing to ensure justice prevailed. His loyalty to his comrades and his determination to protect innocent lives had earned him the respect of his peers.

"He was known for his keen intellect, his resourcefulness, and his ability to adapt to any situation," Hugh added, admiration evident in his voice. "He was one of the best in the field, Elizabeth, and if anyone can help us unravel this intricate web of espionage, it's Daniel."

'It's strange that I've never heard of him', Elizabeth said

'You certainly should have, maybe once or twice. Well, Daniel Carter's history is a little complicated.' Hugh took a deep breath, the weight of the revelation evident in his expression. "During the height of the Cold War," he began, his voice filled with a mixture of gravity and purpose.

"Daniel Carter, your father, and a team of exceptional operatives were tasked with exposing a Soviet Union spy gang that had infiltrated our police and military systems. Their mission went beyond mere intelligence gathering; it was to prevent a heinous plot to assassinate the prime minister and a member of the royal family."

Elizabeth leaned in, her attention completely focused on Hugh as he continued.

"Danger lurked around every corner as they pursued the truth, people were silenced, assassinated to cover this plot up. Your father even got demoted. Daniel led the team, which your father was a part of, with an unwavering commitment to protect the nation. They meticulously pieced together the puzzle, unravelling the web of deceit that had been carefully constructed by the spy gang."

Hugh continued, "They exposed moles, double agents, and hidden operatives who had infiltrated the highest echelons of power. It was a race against time to uncover their plans and thwart the impending danger that loomed over our country."

"The operation culminated in a dramatic takedown," Hugh continued, a glimmer of admiration in his eyes. "Thanks to Daniel's leadership and the unwavering dedication of the team, they exposed the spy gang's intentions, preventing the assassination plot from being carried out. It was a monumental success, a triumph of justice over evil."

The weight of the revelation settled on Elizabeth's shoulders. The sacrifices her father had made, the risks he had taken to ensure the safety of the prime minister and the royal family, were now part of her own story. She felt a deep connection to the legacy.

Still, she felt a weight of dissatisfaction in her, Elizabeth leaned forward, her eyes searching Hugh's face. "Where is

Daniel Carter now?" she asked, her voice laced with anticipation.

Hugh sighed "I'm afraid no one knows his whereabouts at the moment. After the successful exposure of the Soviet Union spy gang and the prevention of the assassination plot, something unexpected happened. Daniel was unjustly arrested."

"Arrested? But he was a hero! Why would they do that?" Elizabeth's eyes widened in disbelief.

"It was a dark time, Elizabeth. The spy gang had connections that ran deep within the system. They were able to manipulate the evidence and paint Daniel as a traitor. They wanted to silence him, to bury the truth, destroy him totally and protect their own interests." Hugh's eyes glowed in the dark as he spoke.

'So he gave it all up for nothing. He sacrificed so much for us, only to be betrayed and arrested by those he had fought against?"

Hugh nodded, his voice filled with empathy. "Yes, it was a grave injustice. The same system he had dedicated his life to defending turned against him. He was imprisoned for years, his name tarnished, and his sacrifices forgotten by those who should have stood by him."

As Hugh continued, his voice filled with a mix of sadness and remorse. "Elizabeth, the years Daniel spent unjustly imprisoned took a heavy toll on him. He endured unimaginable hardships, not just physically, but emotionally as well. He suffered numerous losses during that time, which deeply affected him."

Elizabeth's heart ached at the thought of the pain Daniel must have endured.

Hugh's eyes grew distant as he spoke. "First, there was his secretary, someone he cared for deeply. They had developed a close bond, a trusted partnership built on years of working together. She was killed in his house while he was away. It would appear his enemies came for him and met her.'

Elizabeth's tried to comprehend the magnitude of the emotional upheaval Daniel must have endured. The weight of the injustices piled upon him seemed unbearable.

Hugh continued, this time with a small faint smile at the edge of his lips. She knew Hugh gave this expression when he felt so much he could only contain it with a small smile. “Daniel also lost his assistant, someone he had taken under his wing. She was a bright and promising young operative, full of potential. The loss of her presence in his life further deepened his anguish and isolation."

Elizabeth felt a pang of sadness, imagining the loneliness and despair that Daniel must have felt.

"As the years went by," Hugh continued, his voice growing softer, "Daniel became more withdrawn. He withdrew into himself, shutting out the world and refusing to speak to anyone. The pain and trauma he endured during his time in jail seemed to have broken his spirit."

"It's heartbreaking to think of what he went through," Elizabeth said sadly. "To have his achievements overshadowed by his own wrongful imprisonment and then to suffer such losses while being isolated from the world..."

Hugh nodded quietly "Yes, Elizabeth. The years of silence and solitude left deep scars on Daniel's soul.'

That moment as Elizabeth's mind raced with thoughts of Daniel's suffering and the injustices he had endured, a troubling realization crept into her thoughts. She couldn't help but consider the possibility that Daniel might be harbouring a deep-seated resentment and seeking revenge against Reinhardt and even her own father.

Her heart sank at the thought. She had always regarded her father as a hero, someone who had dedicated his life to protecting the country. But what her father's abandonment of Daniel when he was wrongfully arrested could have triggered Daniel to take his revenge on him, killing him the way he did. The weight of that possibility bore heavily on her.

Elizabeth turned to Hugh, her expression filled with concern. "Hugh, what if Daniel holds a grudge against Reinhardt and my father? After everything he's been through, it's understandable if he seeks revenge.'

Hugh's face tensed with worry as he contemplated Elizabeth's words. "We cannot dismiss the possibility that Daniel might harbour resentment. His experiences have undoubtedly left scars, and it's natural for him to feel a sense of injustice. But that seems most unlikely"

Elizabeth's voice trembled as she continued, "Daniel seeking revenge, could not only have placed Reinhardt at risk but also my father.'

Hugh shook his head, his expression serious. "You have to remember that Daniel was a man of integrity and honour. Yes, his suffering might have fueled anger and bitterness. But I believe there was still goodness in him.'

As the thought of seeking more information about Daniel Carter crossed Elizabeth's mind. She realized that her grandmother, Nana, might hold valuable insights into her father's past and his friendship with Daniel. She turned to Hugh quickly and shared her idea.

"She has always been the closest to my dad. Even more than my mum sometimes. If anyone can shed light on who Daniel Carter is and his relationship with my father, it's her."

Hugh nodded in agreement.

That evening, Elizabeth made her way to Nana's house, her anticipation growing with each step. The sun was setting, casting a warm glow over the neighbourhood as she approached the familiar front porch. She rang the doorbell, and a few moments later, Nana opened the door with a smile.

"Elizabeth, my dear!" Nana exclaimed, her eyes lighting up with joy. "How wonderful to see you. Come in, come in. I've just made a fresh pot of tea."

Elizabeth stepped inside, feeling a sense of comfort wash over her as she entered Nana's cosy home. The familiar scent of tea and Nana's warm presence immediately made her feel at ease. They settled in the living room, cups of tea in hand, and engaged in light-hearted small talk for a while, allowing the warmth of their bond to fill the room.

As the small talk flowed, Elizabeth mustered the courage to bring up the topic that brought her there. She took a deep breath and spoke with earnestness. "Nana, I wanted to ask you about Daniel Carter. I've heard that he was a close friend of Dad's during his time in the intelligence world. Can you share more about him?"

Nana's warm smile faded slightly, and a flicker of discomfort passed through her eyes. She placed her tea cup down gently on the saucer and took a deep breath. Elizabeth sensed the hesitation, realizing that this might be a sensitive topic for Nana. But she also understood that Nana felt a responsibility to provide her with the clarity she sought.

"Elizabeth, my dear," Nana began, her voice tinged with a mix of sadness and resolve, yet she managed to smile 'He was a remarkable man, Elizabeth. He and your father were close acquaintances while he was in the police force.'

Curiosity burned within her, Elizabeth leaned forward "What was he like, Nana? How did he and Dad become such close friends?"

'Ah, Liz. Why are we talking about Daniel Carter? Tell me about your case and the progress you've made so far.'

'No, Nan, this is quite important to the case.' Elizabeth said with a flicker of determination in her eyes.

Nana sighed. "Daniel was a man of unyielding loyalty and courage. He had a sharp mind and a keen eye for detail, which made him an exceptional operative. But it was his unwavering dedication to justice and his unwavering friendship that truly set him apart."

Elizabeth hung on Nana's every word, captivated by the image of Daniel that was taking shape in her mind.

"Nana, was there anything particular about Daniel that stood out to you?" Elizabeth asked, her voice filled with curiosity.

Nana's expression grew weary, her gaze drifting into the distance. "I dunno, Liz. Well, there was something about Daniel's character that always impressed me," she said. "He had a quiet strength, a depth of compassion that ran deep. Despite the dangers they faced, he remained grounded, always mindful of the human side of the work they were doing. Your father spoke so well of him"

Elizabeth nodded, taking in Nana's words. She couldn't help but wonder how Daniel's experiences had shaped him, especially considering the hardships and injustice he had endured.

"Nana," Elizabeth hesitated before continuing, "Do you know what happened to Daniel after his time in the intelligence world? I've heard that he was unjustly arrested."

Nana's face clouded with sadness, and she let out a sigh. "Yes, my dear, I'm afraid that is true. Daniel faced an unimaginable injustice. After his commendable service,'

Elizabeth nodded, her eyes fixed on Nana's face, conveying her understanding and appreciation for the difficulty of the situation. "I know it might be hard for you to talk about, Nana," she said gently, "but I feel that understanding Daniel's journey is essential for me to uncover the truth and seek justice."

Taking a moment to gather her thoughts, Nana continued, her voice filled with a mix of determination and caution. "After their successful mission in exposing the spy gang with your dad, Daniel's life took an unexpected turn. He was wrongly accused and arrested, his name tarnished by those who sought to silence him. It was a grave injustice, Elizabeth, one that your dad did all he could to prevent but couldn't."

Elizabeth's heart sank, feeling a renewed surge of empathy and anger at the injustices Daniel had endured. She held Nana's hand tightly, seeking solace and strength in their connection.

"He suffered greatly, my dear. Isolated from those who cared for him, Daniel faced unimaginable hardships. The loss of dear friends and allies, the betrayal of the very system he had served, it all took a toll on his spirit.

Nana lifted up her eyes and saw the concern in Elizabeth's eyes. She understood the weight of her words. She leaned in closer, her voice filled with reassurance and love.

"Elizabeth, my dear, I want you to know that Daniel Carter was not responsible for your father's death," Nana said firmly, her words carrying the weight of truth. "Yes, there were times when your father spoke of Daniel's shady or shadowy behaviour after his release from jail, but it was never in connection to any harm towards him. They may have had disagreements, but Daniel would never hurt your dad. Your father believed in the goodness within Daniel, despite his struggles."

Elizabeth felt a mixture of relief and confusion wash over her. She had trusted her father's judgment and his belief in Daniel's character. Nana's words provided a sense of comfort, knowing that the friendship between her father and Daniel had endured. But it still didn't feel enough for her.

"Nana, I've been uncovering some disturbing information about the events that led to Daniel's arrest," Elizabeth confessed, her voice filled with concern. "I fear that his suffering might have fueled a desire for revenge against those who wronged him, including Reinhardt and possibly my father. I want to help him find justice, but I also want to ensure the safety of those involved."

Nana's expression softened, and she squeezed Elizabeth's hand gently. "My dear, I understand your concerns, and your desire for justice is admirable. But we must approach this with caution and seek the truth without jumping to conclusions. Daniel's experiences have undoubtedly left scars, but that does not mean he is seeking revenge. We must remember the goodness within him and give him a chance to heal."

Nana took a deep breath, her gaze fixed on a distant memory. "Though, after his release from prison, it was strange. It was like he became a totally different person. He shut off from the world, changed his identity and disappear completely."

Nana continued, "For years, no one heard anything from him. It would seem he was dead. Daniel lived in the shadows. But the last time I heard from him was when one day, your father told me he appeared at his office unannounced.'

'What did he come for?'

'It would seem he had learned of a danger that loomed over Mason and felt compelled to warn him."

Elizabeth leaned forward, captivated by the story unfolding before her. "What kind of danger, Nana? Why did he feel the need to warn Dad?"

Nana's eyes grew distant as she recalled the intensity of that day. "I dunno, Lizzy. I don't. Your father wasn't clear on the details.'

A shiver ran down Elizabeth's spine as she contemplated the magnitude of the danger her father had faced.

"And what did Dad do when Daniel warned him?" Elizabeth finally asked, her voice filled with a mixture of curiosity and concern.

Nana smiled softly, but her brows furrowing with concern. "Your father, Liz...your father was always a man of action, but he trusted quite a lot of people he shouldn't have. Daniel's warning didn't resonate with him as deeply as it should have. He was more concerned about this new enigmatic Daniel that had appeared in his office.

Elizabeth felt a weight of disappointment.

"Nana, did Dad ever find Daniel?" Elizabeth asked, her voice tinged with both hope and worry.

Nana's face softened, and she sighed gently. "No, my dear. Despite his best efforts, Mason wasn't able to locate Daniel. He searched tirelessly, following leads and investigating every possible clue, but it seemed as though Daniel had vanished once again, leaving no trace behind."

As Elizabeth sat in the cosy warmth of Nana's apartment, her heart sank as the weight of the unknown hung heavy in the air. She couldn't help but feel a mix of emotions swirling within her. The information Nana had shared had shed new light on the enigmatic figure of Daniel Carter, but it had also deepened the complexity of her father's death. The realisation that Daniel might not be directly responsible for her father's demise left her feeling both enlightened and confused.

On one hand, Elizabeth now understood that Daniel had resurfaced in her father's life to issue a warning, indicating that he possessed vital information about a danger Mason faced. This suggested that he had a vested interest in protecting her father, not harming him. It raised the question of who was truly responsible for Mason's death and what exactly Daniel had been trying to prevent.

However, the confusion lingered, as the pieces of the puzzle still pointed towards Daniel's involvement. The shadowy nature of his past, the warning he had given, and his subsequent disappearance created an air of suspicion. Elizabeth couldn't ignore the fact that her investigation had led her to Daniel and the belief that he held crucial answers.

Sipping her tea, Elizabeth contemplated the enigma that was Daniel Carter. She realised that her journey would require her to navigate through layers of secrecy and deception to uncover the truth. It was a daunting task, but one she couldn't ignore. She owed it to her father's memory and to herself to unearth the complete story behind his death.

In her mind, she began to piece together the fragments of information, trying to find the missing links that could connect the dots. She was determined to approach this investigation ruthlessly, considering all possibilities and not allowing preconceived notions to cloud her judgement.

The warmth of the room contrasted with the chill she felt in her heart. The weight of responsibility settled upon her shoulders, reminding her that she was venturing into dangerous territory.

As the rain continued to pour outside, Elizabeth realised that she had embarked on a journey that went far beyond seeking justice for her father. She was unravelling a web of secrets that extended beyond her own personal loss. There were greater forces at play, and Daniel Carter was a significant piece of the puzzle.

Elizabeth took a sip of tea while her mind was consumed by thoughts of the two enigmatic figures in her life - Daniel Carter and David Scarlett. The more she delved into their backgrounds and connections, the more she realised that the lines between them were beginning to blur in her mind.

Both Daniel Carter and David Scarlett had a history in the world of espionage. They had served in the police force, their paths crossing in the murky realm of covert operations. Elizabeth couldn't help but wonder if their paths had intertwined more deeply than she initially thought.

The similarities between the two men were striking. They possessed an air of mystery and were associated with dangerous individuals like Reinhardt and Peter Bashir. Elizabeth couldn't shake the feeling that there was a hidden link connecting Daniel and David, one that ran deeper than their shared world of espionage.

Daniel had resurfaced in her father's life, warning him of impending danger. Meanwhile, David Scarlett had been a constant presence in her investigation. The more Elizabeth dug into their backgrounds, the more she realised that these two figures held a significant place in the web of intrigue.

She couldn't ignore the possibility that Daniel and David had operated within the same circles. They were both associated with dangerous men like Reinhardt and Peter Bashir, perhaps even sharing a common mission or objective. The thought sent shivers down her spine. Could it be that the events leading to her father's death were part of a larger game, where the boundaries between allies and enemies blurred?

Elizabeth recalled the conversations she had overheard, the pieces of information that had led her down this tangled path. The Russian spy, the secret codes, the infiltration of nuclear facilities - all of these elements pointed towards a grander scheme, one that involved powerful players and high-stakes consequences.

She pondered the implications of her discoveries. If Daniel and David were indeed connected, then it raised the question of who was pulling the strings and what their ultimate agenda was. Was there a hidden alliance operating behind the scenes, manipulating events to serve their own interests?

The rain continued to fall, mirroring the tumultuous thoughts swirling in Elizabeth's mind. She felt a sense of urgency, the need to untangle these numerous threads of deception

Elizabeth knew that she had to confront the blurred lines between Daniel Carter and David Scarlett. Whatever it might be. She had to peel back the layers of secrecy and discover the connections that bound them together.

While Elizabeth contemplated, a sobbing sound brought her back to the tea-scented warmth of her grandmother's house. It was Nana sobbing. That moment Elizabeth heard was a delicate symphony of sorrow and despair. It was a sound that echoed with a deep emotional resonance, carrying the weight of a lifetime's worth of pain and grief. Each sob seemed to pierce through the air, evoking a sense of vulnerability and heartache.

Elizabeth's heart clenched as she rushed to Nana's side. She found her sitting on the couch, her frail form trembling with the intensity of her emotions. Tears streamed down her wrinkled cheeks, her sobs shaking her entire being.

"Nana, what's wrong?" Elizabeth asked softly, her voice filled with concern. The sound of Nana's crying tore at her heart. She sat beside her, wrapping her arms around Nana's trembling shoulders, offering a gentle embrace of comfort and support. She stroked Nana's silvery hair, trying to soothe her distress.

Nana's sobs continued, making it difficult for her to speak. Between gasps for air, she managed to utter broken words of anguish. "It's... it's Mason. He... he's gone. My son's gone."

Elizabeth's breath caught in her throat as her mind raced to comprehend Nana's words. Nana sat there on the couch, her fragile frame hunched over, consumed by an overwhelming sorrow that seemed to seep from the very depths of her being. Her eyes, usually bright and full of life, were now red and swollen from the countless tears that cascaded down her weathered cheeks.

She tried to hide her tears, hastily wiping them away with the tip of her sleeve, as if afraid to reveal her vulnerability. But the grief that engulfed her was too immense to be contained, and the tears continued to flow, leaving a trail of dampness in their wake.

Her face, etched with lines and wrinkles earned through a lifetime of experience, looked weary and worn. The weight of the world seemed to bear down on her shoulders, causing her body to tremble with each sob that escaped her lips. Her once vibrant spirit was now overshadowed by an undeniable sense of loss and despair.

Nana's silver hair, usually neatly arranged, now appeared dishevelled and unkempt. Strands clung to her tear-streaked face, accentuating the rawness of her emotions. As the rain continued to patter against the windows, its gentle rhythm providing a backdrop to her sorrow, Nana seemed to become smaller, more fragile, in the face of her grief.

Her hands, once steady and capable, now shook with each sob. She clutched the tip of her sweater tightly in her grasp, its fabric becoming saturated with her tears. She tried to compose herself, to regain her composure, but the weight of her sadness proved too great, and she succumbed to the overwhelming pain that consumed her.

The room, once filled with warmth and light, now seemed to mirror Nana's anguish. Shadows danced upon the walls, their movements mirroring the turbulent emotions within her. The soft glow of the lamp cast a gentle halo around her, emphasising the vulnerability and fragility of the moment.

Elizabeth, witnessing her Nana's profound grief, felt her own heart ache in sympathy. She longed to ease the burden that weighed so heavily upon her grandmother's frail shoulders, to offer solace and support in this time of immense sadness. She moved closer, her own tears glistening in her eyes as she reached out to gently caress Nana's trembling hand.

"Nana," Elizabeth whispered, her voice filled with love and concern, "you don't have to bear this pain alone. I'm here for you."

As the echoes of their shared silence lingered in the room, Nana's tears gradually subsided, leaving behind trails of sorrow on her weathered cheeks. Nana finally found her voice, her words punctuated by the weight of her fear and concern. Her voice trembled as she spoke, her words carrying a mix of sorrow, love, and a profound sense of protection.

"Elizabeth," Nana began, her voice quivering with emotion, "I have lived through moments of unimaginable loss and witnessed the sacrifices your father made to protect what he believed in. And now, I see that same fire burning within you. It both fills me with pride and terrifies me."

Her eyes, still teary and red from the onslaught of tears, locked with Elizabeth's gaze. The room seemed to hold its breath, the air heavy with the weight of their shared vulnerability.

"I'm scared for you, my dear," Nana continued, her voice barely above a whisper. "I fear that you will follow in your father's footsteps, that you will go to great lengths to protect what you care about, even if it means sacrificing yourself in the process."

Elizabeth's heart ached at the raw honesty and love in her Nana's words.

"I don't want to lose you, Elizabeth," Nana confessed, her voice filled with a mixture of sadness and determination. "Your father's death was a painful blow to me, and I don't know if I could bear losing you in the same way."

Tears welled up in Elizabeth's eyes, mirroring the emotions that danced across her Nana's face. She reached out, taking hold of her grandmother's weathered hands, feeling the warmth and strength within them.

Nana's grip tightened around Elizabeth's hands, a mixture of fear and pride evident in her eyes. She knew her granddaughter's heart was set on a path of truth and justice, and she couldn't deny the fire that burned within her.

"I know, my dear," Nana whispered, her voice tinged with both sadness and resilience. "I know I can't stop you from pursuing your truth, just as I couldn't stop your father. But...' Nana's tears returned.

As Nana's sobs grew louder, her tears flowed freely, and her body shook with the weight of her emotions. Elizabeth sat beside her, feeling the heaviness in her own heart as she listened to the raw anguish pouring forth from her grandmother's soul.

"I see so much of your father in you, Elizabeth," Nana choked out between sobs, her voice filled with a mix of pain and regret. "The way you refuse to back down, the determination that fuels your every step... It's a reminder of him, of the passion that consumed him."

Elizabeth's throat tightened as she absorbed Nana's words. That moment brought a stark and a painful reminder of the void left by her father's absence. She had always admired him, and looked up to him as a beacon of strength and integrity. And now, she found herself unwittingly dug in the depth of grief of his demise again by watching her grandmother cry about him...

"I wish your father hadn't met such a tragic end," Nana continued, her voice breaking with the weight of her sorrow. "I wish he could have witnessed the remarkable person you've become. But life has a cruel way of snatching away our loved ones.

Tears streamed down Elizabeth's face, mirroring the profound grief etched upon Nana's features. She reached out, her hand trembling, and gently brushed away a tear from her grandmother's cheek.

"I wish he was here too, Nana," Elizabeth whispered, her voice filled with longing and sadness. Overwhelmed by the depth of their shared emotions, Elizabeth couldn't help but feel a surge of empathy and sorrow. Her own tears mingled with Nana's, as grief, love, and longing filled the room. She gently embraced her grandmother, pulling her close, seeking solace in their shared embrace.

They held each other tightly, their bodies trembling with the weight of their emotions. Elizabeth's hand tenderly patted Nana's back, offering a soothing rhythm as she whispered words of comfort and reassurance.

"It's okay, Nana," Elizabeth whispered, her voice choked with emotion. "We'll get through this together. We'll honour Dad's memory, and we won't let his sacrifices be in vain."

Nana clung to her granddaughter, finding solace in the warmth of her embrace. Her tears soaked Elizabeth's shoulder, and the room seemed to fill with the echoes of their shared sorrow.

"I miss him so much," Nana whispered, her voice trembling with raw vulnerability. "I miss his laughter, his wisdom, and the way he always knew how to bring light into the darkest of moments."

Elizabeth's heart ached, the weight of her own grief resurfacing in the wake of Nana's words. Memories of her father flooded her mind, moments frozen in time, etched deep within her soul.

"I miss him too, Nana," Elizabeth replied, her voice filled with a mix of sadness and pain.

As the sobs subsided, their grip on each other loosened, but the connection remained strong. Elizabeth reached out, gently wiping away

Nana's tears, her touch filled with tenderness and understanding.

Elizabeth stepped out from the warmth of Nana's house into the cold London Street. The rain had finally ceased, leaving London Street glistening under the soft glow of streetlights. She tightened the collar of her coat around her neck, warding off the chill that lingered in the night air.

The city seemed to hold its breath as Elizabeth made her way through its labyrinthine streets. The occasional passerby hurried past, their faces shielded from the world, lost in their own thoughts and worries.

Lost in her thoughts, Elizabeth found herself walking down familiar streets, ones she had roamed countless times before. Thinking of just one thing; her father...

A gentle breeze swept through the streets, carrying with it the distant sound of laughter and music, reminders of a world that existed beyond the shadows she now found herself immersed in. But she pressed on, her determination pushing her forward.

As Elizabeth's steps carried her farther into the night, her mind remained occupied with her Nana's words, echoing through the corridors of her thoughts. She couldn't help but contemplate the truth in her grandmother's observations, realising that perhaps her Nana was right about her, at least to some extent.

The parallels between Elizabeth and her father were undeniable. They shared the same passion for uncovering the truth, and the same unwavering determination to protect what they cared about. They had both chosen a path that led them into

Her mind dwelled on her father's memory, bringing forth a realisation that she had suppressed her grief since his tragic death. In the aftermath of his passing, she had thrown herself into her quest for truth, burying her sorrow deep within, and relying on denial to cope with the pain.

But now, as the weight of her Nana's words settled within her, she couldn't ignore the truth any longer. She had been shielding herself from the grief, holding back her tears to appear strong, both for her father and for herself. The walls she had built around her heart were beginning to crack, and the floodgates of sorrow threatened to burst open.

Elizabeth stopped for a moment, her breath catching in her chest. She looked up at the night sky, seeking solace in its vastness, as if the stars held the answers she sought. The realisation hit her with a force she couldn't ignore—the need to confront her grief, to allow herself to feel the pain and loss that had shaped her existence since her father's untimely departure.

Tears welled up in her eyes, shimmering like diamonds in the dim streetlights. She closed her eyes, allowing a single tear to escape, tracing a path down her cheek. The pain, long suppressed, clawed its way to the surface, demanding acknowledgement.

Elizabeth embraced the truth she had been avoiding. The weight of her father's absence, the deep aching in her heart, and the void left by his departure—all crashed upon her like an ocean wave. And she had sort strength in denying her emotions, not allowing herself to fully experience them.

But at that moment, her body trembled as she unleashed her grief, her sobs breaking the silence of the night. The tears flowed freely, unburdening her soul, washing away the facade of strength she had clung to for so long. Each tear brought a loving memory of her dad to her heart.

As soon memories flooded her mind—her father's laughter, his comforting presence, and the way he had guided her through life. The weight of his absence seemed almost unbearable, as if a piece of her had been torn away, leaving an irreparable void.

The rain resumed its steady descent from the heavens above, Elizabeth found herself soaked in its watery embrace. Each droplet mingled with her tears, merging into a torrent of emotions cascading down her face. The cold raindrops mixed with the warmth of her sorrow, created a bittersweet sensation that mirrored the tumultuous storm within her.

As the raindrops mingled with her tears, Elizabeth felt a strange sense of connection with the elements. The rain mirrored her anguish, its cleansing touch soothing her wounded soul. The downpour became a conduit for her grief, carrying it away into the depths of the earth, freeing her from the burden she had carried for so long.

As she walked, her sobs gradually faded into a gentle exhale. However, the rain persisted, a relentless downpour that seemed to mirror the cascade of emotions within Elizabeth. As she stood in the midst of the chilling downpour, the icy droplets pierced through her clothing, instantly dampening her skin and sending shivers down her spine.

The air was heavy with moisture, the misty rain clinging to her like a shroud. Each raindrop felt like a tiny pinprick, as if the heavens were testing her resilience. The water seeped through her hair, matting it against her scalp, and plastered her clothes against her body, weighing them down with the added burden of water.

A cold breeze swept through the streets, cutting through the fabric of her clothes and chilling her to the bone. It was a biting cold, one that seemed to penetrate her very being, causing her body to tremble involuntarily. Her teeth chattered, and her limbs felt heavy and numb as the cold worked its way into every crevice.

The raindrops, once warm tears of release, now turned into icy needles that stung her skin with each impact. The water trickled down her face, mingling with her tears, creating a bitter taste on her lips. She hugged herself tightly, desperately seeking warmth within her own embrace, but it provided little solace against the biting cold.

Her fingers, once nimble and dexterous, now felt stiff and clumsy as the cold gnawed at them. They became pale and lifeless, lacking the usual warmth that brought comfort and ease. It was as if the frigid touch of the rain had drained away the vitality and energy that coursed through her veins.

Her body, once vibrant and resilient, now felt vulnerable and fragile in the face of the merciless elements. Each step she took seemed to echo with a dull ache, as if her very bones were being chilled from within. The ground beneath her feet became slick and slippery, making her movements cautious and deliberate.

As the rain fell incessantly, the world around her seemed to lose its colours, muted by the greyness of the sky and the dimness of the day. The streets appeared desolate and sombre, with only the occasional figure scurrying past, seeking refuge from the unyielding rain. The city itself seemed to hunker down under the weight of the downpour, as if nature itself had conspired to mirror the depths of her sorrow.

As Elizabeth hurried through the rain-soaked streets, her mind focused on one destination - Hugh's house. With each step, her determination grew stronger, fueled by a desire for solace and understanding. The familiar route seemed longer under the weight of her emotions, but she pressed on, driven by a sense of urgency.

The rain continued to pour, drenching her further, but she paid little attention to her own discomfort. Her thoughts were consumed by the need to find Hugh.

Finally, she reached Hugh's house, the sight of its familiar facade providing a small measure of comfort. She rang the doorbell, her heart pounding with a mixture of anxiety and anticipation. The door swung open, revealing Hugh standing before her, concern etched across his face as he took in her dishevelled appearance.

Without a word, Elizabeth stepped inside, welcomed by the warmth of the house. Hugh closed the door behind her, shutting out the sound of the rain and creating a sanctuary from the storm outside. The cosy interior provided a stark contrast to the relentless down

Hugh, who had just gotten out of bed in his pyjamas, was taken aback by the unexpected sight of Elizabeth standing before him, cold and wet from the relentless rain. His eyebrows furrowed with concern as he quickly realised the urgency in her presence. Without hesitation, he hurriedly guided her into the house, his hand reaching out to steady her as she stepped over the threshold.

Elizabeth shivered, both from the chill in the air and the overwhelming emotions that had brought her to Hugh's doorstep. She wrapped her arms around herself, seeking some semblance of warmth and comfort. Hugh, sensing her need, disappeared briefly into another room before returning with a soft, warm blanket in his hands.

"Here, take this," he said gently, draping the blanket over her shoulders. "It'll help keep you warm. Come, let's get you out of those wet clothes." His voice carried a soothing tone, a reassurance that she was safe in his presence.

He led her to a nearby couch, where she sat down gratefully, the blanket providing a cocoon of warmth. Hugh disappeared into the kitchen, the sound of running water and clinking dishes indicating his preparations. Moments later, he returned with a steaming cup of tea, the comforting aroma wafting through the room.

"Here, drink this," he said, placing the cup in her trembling hands. "It'll help warm you up from the inside." His eyes held a mix of concern and care as he watched her take a sip, the warmth spreading through her body, chasing away the chill that had settled within her.

As she sipped the tea, the steam rising in delicate tendrils, Elizabeth couldn't help but feel a sense of gratitude towards Hugh. His presence and his actions were a balm to her wounded soul, providing a much-needed respite from the storm that raged both within and outside of her. Hugh seeing she had finished her cup, rushed back to the kitchen to get her a refill.

As Elizabeth sat on the couch, shivering from the cold, she couldn't help but notice Hugh's presence. His large black and red pyjamas hung loosely on his tall frame, accentuating his broad shoulders and strong physique. The colours of his attire seemed to mirror the intensity of the moment.

As he moved around the kitchen, his pyjama shirt slightly unbuttoned, Elizabeth's gaze was drawn to his chest. The sight of his sleek abs and the gentle rise and fall of his breathing stirred something within her. There was a raw and captivating appeal about him that she couldn't deny.

Hugh's movements were confident and graceful, a reflection of his self-assured nature. His blonde hair was slightly tousled, as if he had just woken up, giving him an effortlessly attractive aura. The soft glow of the kitchen lights illuminated his features, highlighting his chiseled jawline and captivating hazel eyes.

There was a sense of calm and warmth that radiated from Hugh as he prepared the tea. The way he moved with purpose and precision, his hands gracefully handling the cups and the teapot, showed a level of comfort and familiarity in the kitchen. It was as if he had a natural talent for creating a soothing atmosphere.

Elizabeth couldn't help but be captivated by his presence. It wasn't just his physical appearance that drew her in; it was the way he carried himself with a quiet confidence and kindness. His presence felt comforting, like a shelter from the storm that had been raging within her.

As he poured the hot water into the teacup, a small smile played at the corners of his lips.

She found herself mesmerized by the way he effortlessly balanced strength and gentleness. There was an air of mystery about him, an untold story lurking beneath the surface. It was as if he held secrets and experiences that had shaped him into the person he was today.

Hugh's presence in the kitchen was a balm for Elizabeth's weary soul. Hugh approached her with another warm cup of tea and sat with her. At that moment, as they sat together, Elizabeth couldn't help but feel a sense of gratitude for Hugh's unwavering support. The warmth of the tea radiated through her, matching the warmth she felt in her heart. She realized that sometimes, comfort and solace could be found in unexpected places and with unexpected people.

As they sat in his living room, Elizabeth couldn't help but appreciate the warmth of the moment. The rain continued to fall outside, creating a soothing rhythm that echoed their inner thoughts. And at that moment, surrounded by warmth and understanding, Elizabeth knew that she had found a safe haven in Hugh's presence.

The silence between them felt comfortable, a refuge from the outside world. Hugh moved closer to her, his presence offering a sense of companionship that was both comforting and grounding. He waited patiently, allowing Elizabeth the space she needed to gather her thoughts and find the words to express the turmoil within her.

Finally, as the warmth from the tea began to seep into her bones, Elizabeth turned to Hugh, her voice barely above a whisper. "I... I needed to see you," she admitted, her eyes glistening with tears.

Hugh's expression softened, his gaze filled with empathy. He reached out, his hand gently covering hers. "It's okay, Elizabeth," he said softly. "I'm here for you, just as I've always been."

At that moment, Elizabeth felt a glimmer of hope. The weight that had burdened her for so long seemed a little lighter, knowing that she had someone like Hugh by her side. As the rain continued to tap against the windows, she knew that she had taken the first step towards finding solace

As Hugh sat beside her, his strong arms encircled Elizabeth in a comforting embrace. The warmth of his body pressed against hers, sending a soothing sensation through her chilled frame. In that embrace, she felt a sense of security and reassurance, as if all the worries and burdens of the world were momentarily lifted.

They sat there in silence, finding solace in each other's presence. Words seemed unnecessary in that moment of shared understanding. The gentle rhythm of their breaths and the beating of their hearts spoke volumes, conveying a depth of connection that surpassed any spoken language.

Elizabeth nestled closer to Hugh, finding solace in his embrace. She could feel the steady rise and fall of his chest against her back, a comforting reminder that they were both alive and breathing in sync with one another. The sound of the rain outside provided a gentle backdrop, a natural melody that seemed to lull them into a state of tranquillity.

In that silent embrace, Elizabeth felt a sense of acceptance and belonging. It was as if the world outside ceased to exist, and all that mattered was the warmth they shared in that small kitchen. The weight of her grief and confusion slowly lifted, replaced by a newfound sense of peace.

She allowed herself to fully surrender to the healing power of their embrace. The tears she had held back earlier now flowed freely, mingling with the rain that continued to fall outside. It was a cathartic release, a necessary step towards healing and embracing the truth of her father's tragic death.

They remained in that embrace for what felt like an eternity, finding solace in the simplicity of their connection. Elizabeth felt a profound gratitude for Hugh's presence, for his willingness to be there for her in her time of need. It was a reminder that love and comfort could be found in the arms of someone who truly cared.

As time passed, the silence between them began to speak louder than any words ever could. It was a language of understanding, compassion, and shared vulnerability. They didn't need to talk about the pain or the challenges they faced; their mere presence and the comfort they found in each other's arms was enough.

As their bodies pressed against each other, the heat they shared seemed to permeate every fibre of their beings. It was more than just the physical warmth of their bodies; it was an emotional and spiritual connection that radiated from within. At that moment, the world outside ceased to exist, and all that mattered was the love they held for each other.

The warmth seeped into Elizabeth's bones, thawing away the chill of the night and the burdens she carried. It was as if a protective cocoon had been formed around them, shielding them from the harsh realities of the outside world. In that sacred space, time seemed to stand still, allowing them to bask in the tranquillity of their love.

The sensation of warmth extended beyond their physical bodies. It was an intangible feeling, a profound sense of security and belonging that transcended the limits of the tangible world. As they held each other, Elizabeth felt a sense of peace wash over her, melting away the worries and anxieties that had plagued her heart.

As Elizabeth rested her head against Hugh's chest, she could hear the steady rhythm of his heartbeat. It was a lullaby, a gentle reminder of the life and love that pulsed within him. The sound reverberated through her, resonating with her own heartbeat, as if they were dancing to the same beautiful melody.

As the night wore on, they remained embraced, savouring the precious moments of togetherness. The rain continued to fall outside, a gentle symphony that provided a backdrop to their intimate connection. The warmth they shared became a sanctuary, a refuge from the cold and harsh realities of the world.

In that smudge feeling of warmth, Elizabeth knew she was exactly where she was meant to be. In Hugh's arms, away from the cold and rain, she found a sense of home. And as they held each other, surrounded by the serenity of the night, their love became an eternal flame that would keep them warm, even in the coldest of nights.

CHAPTER EIGHT: TWO-FACED

The next day. Elizabeth woke up and took Hugh's car to the cemetery. She got out of the car with flowers and walked in through the gates of the cemetery, her steps measured and purposeful. The air was crisp, carrying a faint scent of earth and dampness. The morning sunlight filtered through the clouds, casting a soft glow upon the rows of tombstones that stretched out before her.

She made her way along the winding paths, her eyes scanning the names etched in stone. The silence enveloped her, broken only by the distant chirping of birds and the rustle of leaves in the gentle breeze. Each step brought her closer to her destination, a familiar spot that held both sorrow and solace.

As she approached her father's grave, a mixture of emotions swelled within her. Grief mingled with a profound sense of love and longing. The marble headstone stood tall, a sombre reminder of the loss she had endured. She knelt down, placing the bouquet of flowers gently at the base of the grave.

Her fingers traced the engraved letters of her Mason Morgan, as if seeking a connection beyond the confines of mortality. Memories flooded her mind, moments shared, laughter and tears, the lessons imparted. She closed her eyes, allowing herself to be consumed by the wave of emotions that washed over her.

Yet, the stillness of the cemetery seemed to hold her grief, absorbing it like a solemn witness. The trees swayed gently, as if offering a silent comfort, while the distant sound of leaves rustling soothed her troubled soul. She took solace in the knowledge that she was not alone in her pain, that countless others had stood in this very place, seeking solace and connection.

As time passed, Elizabeth felt a sense of release, a lightening of the burden she had carried within her. She knew that her father's physical presence may be gone, but his love and guidance remained etched within her heart. The cemetery became a sacred space where she could commune with his memory, finding strength in the bond they shared.

Elizabeth sat in front of her father's gravestone, enveloped by the serene atmosphere of the cemetery. The air was hushed, carrying a sense of reverence that seemed to permeate every corner. The stillness wrapped around her like a gentle embrace, offering solace and space for contemplation.

The cemetery seemed like a sanctuary, a place where time stood still and the worries of the world faded away. The tall trees surrounding the area swayed gracefully in the breeze, their leaves whispering secrets of the past. Sunlight filtered through the branches, casting dappled shadows on the ground, creating a dance of light and shade.

Birds perched on the branches, their melodic songs filling the air with sweet melodies. Their voices seemed to carry a message of hope and renewal, a reminder that life continued even in the face of loss. Elizabeth closed her eyes, allowing herself to be immersed in the symphony of nature, finding solace in the harmonious notes that surrounded her.

The scent of blooming flowers wafted through the air, a gentle reminder of the cycle of life and the beauty that emerged from even the darkest moments. Soft petals adorned nearby graves, a vibrant burst of colour against the backdrop of the solemn cemetery. Elizabeth breathed in the delicate fragrance, feeling a sense of connection to the natural world and the inherent cycles of existence.

As she sat in silence, she became aware of the subtle sounds that often go unnoticed. The distant rustling of leaves, the chirping of insects, and the soft murmur of a nearby stream. These gentle whispers of nature seemed to offer a sense of comfort, reminding her that she was part of a greater tapestry, interconnected with all living things.

Time seemed suspended in this moment of reflection, as if the outside world had faded away, leaving only Elizabeth and her father's presence. The serenity of the cemetery offered a sanctuary for her grief, a place where she could find solace and draw strength from the forces of nature and the memories of her father.

As the forces of nature embraced her in their gentle embrace, leaving her with a renewed spirit and a deeper connection to her father's memory. She noticed an old man entering the cemetery. He walked with a measured pace, his steps displaying a sense of purpose. In his hands, he carried a vibrant bouquet of flowers, a colourful contrast against the solemn backdrop of the cemetery.

Elizabeth's gaze followed the old man as he made his way through the rows of gravestones. There was a gracefulness in his movements, despite the slight trembling in his aged hands. He seemed deeply focused, his attention directed towards a specific gravestone. Elizabeth watched intently as he gently placed the flowers on the designated spot, tenderly arranging them with care.

The old man stood still for a moment, his gaze fixed upon the gravestone. His weathered face bore a mixture of sorrow and nostalgia, a reflection of the emotions that weighed upon him.

Elizabeth couldn't help but feel a sense of empathy, an unspoken understanding of the significance behind his actions.

As the old man turned away from the gravestone, Elizabeth's gaze lingered on him. There was a certain air of melancholy surrounding him, as if he carried the weight of a lifetime of memories and regrets. He glanced around, his eyes scanning the surroundings, as if searching for a familiar face or a lost connection.

Without exchanging any words, the old man's purpose seemed fulfilled, and he began to make his way back towards the entrance of the cemetery. Elizabeth watched as he walked, his figure gradually fading into the distance. The rain-soaked paths seemed to echo his footsteps, creating a hushed atmosphere that intensified the solitude of the cemetery.

As he reached the edge of the cemetery, a taxi awaited him, its engine idling softly. Just as Elizabeth was about to shift her gaze away, something caught her attention. It was the taxi driver waiting by the entrance of the cemetery. Recognition sparked within her as she realised it was the same taxi driver who had apprehended her on her way to the S.I.S headquarters, warning her to watch her back due to her investigation into David Scarlett.

Her heart raced, and without a second thought, she sprang to her feet, determined to find out more. She hurriedly made her way towards the old man, the damp grass beneath her feet dampening the sound of her steps.

But despite her best efforts, the old man reached the taxi before she could catch up, and they drove off together, leaving Elizabeth in their wake.

A surge of frustration and curiosity coursed through her veins. She quickly returned to her own car, determination burning in her eyes. She knew she couldn't let this opportunity slip through her fingers. Ignoring the rain that had just began to drizzle, she got into her car and started the engine, ready to follow the taxi and uncover the truth that lay hidden beneath the surface.

The pursuit began as Elizabeth trailed the taxi through the winding streets of the city. Her focus intensified, her mind racing with possibilities and theories. She knew she was drawing closer to the answers she sought, and the anticipation built with each passing minute.

As the taxi weaved through traffic, Elizabeth's mind wandered, contemplating the significance of the old man's visit to her father's gravestone. Who was he? And did he hold the key to the truth she had been seeking all along?

However, despite her best efforts, the taxi driver's skills proved to be too elusive. He expertly manoeuvred through the crowded streets, leaving Elizabeth trailing behind. The frustration threatened to consume her, but she refused to give up. She would not let this chance slip away.

The pursuit continued, taking them through familiar streets and unknown corners of the city. Elizabeth's senses heightened as she clung to every detail, hoping for a breakthrough. The rain, which had been a constant presence, mirrored the intensity of her emotions. It seemed as though even the heavens themselves were weeping for the truth that remained just out of her grasp.

Finally, after what felt like an eternity, the taxi abruptly came to a halt. Elizabeth's heart raced with anticipation as she pulled up behind it. The Taxi driver got out of the taxi with a gun in his hands pointed at Elizabeth.

'Get on the floor!' The taxi driver, whose look turned from a casual face to a menacing one, said.

Elizabeth stood there with her hands raised in surrender, her heart raced with a mix of fear and adrenaline. The rain continued to fall, creating a cold and tense atmosphere around them. The taxi driver's face was masked by a look of determination, his grip tight on the gun he held in his hand.

Time seemed to slow down as Elizabeth's gaze remained fixed on the man inside the taxi. She slowly raised her hands, her gaze still locked on the disappearing taxi. She knew that she couldn't back down now. The encounter had only fueled her determination to uncover the truth and bring those responsible to justice.

Taking a deep breath, she made a silent vow to herself to delve deeper into the mysteries that lay ahead. She would not be deterred by threats or intimidation. With renewed determination, Elizabeth turned and walked away from the cemetery, ready to face whatever challenges awaited her on the path to unravelling the truth.

The taxi driver's face contorted from an expression of casual indifference to one of menace and aggression. His eyes narrowed, darkening with a sinister intensity. Every line on his face seemed etched with malevolence, accentuated by the dim light filtering through the rain-soaked air.

His eyes glinted with a cold and calculating intensity. They bore into Elizabeth. The veins on his forehead seemed to pulse with his heightened aggression, adding an unsettling touch to his menacing appearance.

The raindrops seemed to fall with more weight, their patter against the ground echoing the tension that filled the space. Even the surrounding sounds of nature seemed to hush, as if nature itself recognized the danger emanating from the taxi driver.

As the gravity of the situation settled upon her, Elizabeth could feel her heartbeat quicken and her breath become shallow. Elizabeth complied with the taxi driver's command, sinking down onto the cold, damp ground, kneeling.

The rain soon subsided and the man in the taxi opened the door and stepped out.
Her eyes remained fixated on him. To her astonishment, she recognized him immediately—it was Daniel Carter, the enigmatic figure who was a puzzle in her investigation.

Daniel approached with a calm and composed demeanour, his gaze steady and unwavering. There was a certain air of mystery surrounding him, as if he held the answers to the questions that had consumed Elizabeth's thoughts for so long. The rain continued to fall around them, adding a sense of urgency and tension to the encounter.

His presence commanded attention, and Elizabeth couldn't help but notice the strength and confidence radiating from him. He moved with purpose, each step measured and deliberate. The years had etched lines of experience onto his face, lending him an air of wisdom and resilience.

As he drew closer, Elizabeth's eyes locked with his, searching for any signs of recognition or familiarity. She saw a glimmer of something in his gaze—a mixture of curiosity, concern, and perhaps even a hint of recognition.

Daniel's features, though weathered by time, retained a rugged handsomeness. His piercing eyes held a depth that hinted at the experiences he had endured, and his strong jawline suggested a determination that had withstood the test of time. Despite the gravity of the situation, there was an aura of calmness and resilience that surrounded him.

As he reached her side, Daniel stopped, his movements fluid and controlled.

Despite the passage of time, his physical appearance bore no trace of fragility or diminished strength. Instead, he exuded an aura of quiet power and resilience.

His weathered face bore the marks of a life lived on the edge, lines etched deeply into his skin, evidence of experiences that had shaped him. Yet, there was an unmistakable air of vitality that clung to him, as if youth and wisdom coexisted within his being.

His eyes, the windows to his soul, held a captivating blend of intensity and serenity. The stormy grey irises shimmered with a youthful glimmer, defying the notion of age. Within their depths, one could sense a wellspring of knowledge and an understanding that transcended time.

Daniel's countenance was framed by a rugged, salt-and-pepper beard that accentuated his chiselled features. Each hair seemed to possess a story of its own, whispering tales of past adventures and battles fought. His lips, thin and firm, conveyed determination and a steadfast resolve.

Standing at a height that commanded attention, Daniel's posture exuded confidence and a silent strength. His broad shoulders hinted at a physical prowess that belied his age, suggesting a man who had honed both body and mind through a lifetime of dedication and discipline. Muscles, taut and defined, seemed ready to spring into action at a moment's notice, a testament to his unwavering physicality.

Dressed in a dark overcoat that clung to his powerful frame, Daniel exuded an air of timeless elegance and understated sophistication. The rain cascaded down the fabric, leaving trails of moisture in its wake, accentuating the ruggedness of his appearance.

His hands, weathered and calloused, hinted at a life filled with both manual labour and precision. They bore the scars of battles fought, both literal and metaphorical, yet retained a gracefulness that suggested a deep-seated refinement beneath the surface.

In the midst of the encounter, Daniel remained silent, his eyes locked on Elizabeth, conveying a depth of emotion and unspoken understanding. It was as if he possessed an innate ability to communicate without words, drawing her into his world of intrigue and secrets.

With every aspect of his being, Daniel Carter embodied an intriguing juxtaposition—a paradoxical blend of aged wisdom and untamed vitality. His presence commanded attention, and in his silence, he spoke volumes. Elizabeth found herself captivated by the enigma that stood before her.

'Hello, Elizabeth. I'm aware you've been trailing me for a while now.' Daniel said.

Daniel's voice, when it finally broke the silence, held a captivating blend of authority and weariness. His voice, low and reassuring, carried a hint of familiarity that resonated deep within Elizabeth. Each word was carefully measured, as if he had spent years perfecting the art of choosing the right ones.

Elizabeth's heart skipped a beat as she heard her name uttered by Daniel.

There was a calmness in his tone, a sense of knowing that seemed to transcend the current situation.

With a mix of trepidation and curiosity, Elizabeth managed to compose herself enough to respond. "How did you know?"

But Daniel's eyes seemed to bore into her, penetrating the depths of her soul as he studied her reaction. There was a flicker of a knowing smile on his lips, an acknowledgement of their intertwined fates.

Elizabeth looked up at Daniel, her brows furrowed in a deep expression of confusion. Her eyes searched his face for answers, trying to make sense of the enigma before her. The lines on her forehead deepened, accentuating the puzzlement that consumed her features. Her lips parted slightly, as if she wanted to speak, but words eluded her at that moment.

A mix of emotions played across her face, ranging from curiosity to scepticism. She felt a sense of unease, not knowing whether to believe the man who stood before her. His presence had unsettled her, and the weight of the revelations he had alluded to hung heavily in the air.

The confusion in her eyes mirrored the intricate web of thoughts spinning in her mind. She grappled with the conflicting notions of danger and possibility, unsure of the path she should tread. It was as if her world had been turned upside down, and the pieces no longer fit together.

In that pivotal moment, as Elizabeth's gaze locked with Daniel's, a wave of realisation washed over her. The pieces of the puzzle suddenly fell into place, forming a picture she had been relentlessly pursuing for months. The truth hit her like a lightning bolt, illuminating the shadowy corners of her investigation.

David Scarlett, the elusive figure she had been tracking, was Daniel Carter! The shock reverberated through her body, leaving her momentarily breathless. How had she missed the connection? How had she failed to see the truth that had been staring her in the face?

Her mind raced to reconcile the new information with everything she had known so far. The signs had been there, hidden beneath layers of deception and misdirection. The shared history between Daniel and her father, their involvement in espionage, and the dangerous men they had encountered—all the threads had woven a tapestry of secrets she was only beginning to unravel.

As the realisation settled within her, a mix of emotions surged through Elizabeth's veins. There was a surge of adrenaline, a rush of fear mingled with determination. The gravity of the situation weighed heavily on her shoulders, as she now stood face-to-face with the man who held the answers she had sought.

David Scarlett, or rather Daniel Carter, exuded an aura of power and mystery that had captivated her from the start. The lines on his weathered face spoke of a life lived on the edge, of countless battles fought in the shadows. His piercing eyes, once filled with youthful wisdom, now bore the weight of a lifetime of secrets. Elizabeth couldn't help but be both drawn to and wary of him.

The revelation struck her like a tidal wave, challenging everything she thought she knew. The complexities of the situation unfolded before her, like a labyrinth she had unknowingly stepped into. This was no longer a simple investigation—it was a dangerous dance with a man who embodied both danger and intrigue.

As the shocking realisation settled within Elizabeth's mind, it felt as if the ground beneath her feet had shifted. She had spent countless hours poring over files and photographs, building a mental image of David Scarlett. She had imagined him to be a man of youth and vigour, someone who could easily blend into a crowd, effortlessly slipping through the shadows like a modern-day James Bond. But the truth shattered that perception, revealing a stark contrast to her expectations.

The man standing before her, defied the image she had constructed in her mind. He was older, his face etched with lines that spoke of a lifetime of experience. His hair, once dark and lustrous, now showed traces of grey, adding an air of wisdom and weariness. This revelation sent a shockwave through Elizabeth's being, challenging her preconceived notions and forcing her to confront the truth head-on.

As Elizabeth gazed into Daniel's eyes, she saw a depth and intensity that belied his age. Though his physical appearance had changed, the fire within him still burned bright. His gaze held a mixture of wisdom and determination, revealing a man who had weathered storms and emerged stronger on the other side. There was an air of danger and intrigue surrounding him, a magnetic pull that drew Elizabeth in, despite the unsettling nature of their encounter.

This unexpected revelation added another layer of complexity to the situation. Elizabeth had been chasing a mirage, pursuing an idealised version of David Scarlett that had never truly existed. She had been captivated by the idea of a dashing, youthful spy, only to discover that the reality was far more nuanced and enigmatic.

'I have a huge respect for your father. That's the only reason I'll do this.' David Scarlett said

David Scarlett's gaze remained steady, his face betraying no hint of emotion. The weight of his statement hung heavily in the air, stirring a mix of emotions within her.

Immediately Elizabeth felt a dart stuck in her neck, making her feel really dizzy. Her vision blurred and her surroundings began to spin. A wave of dizziness washed over her, causing her to sway unsteadily on her feet. Panic surged through her veins as she instinctively reached up to her neck, feeling the small dart protruding from her skin.

Frantically, Elizabeth looked towards David Scarlett, her eyes filled with a mix of confusion, fear, and accusation. The street spun around her, and her limbs grew heavy and unresponsive. She tried to speak, but her voice came out as a faint whisper, lost in the swirling haze of her mind.

David's face, once enigmatic, now appeared distant and detached.

The room began to fade, as if consumed by an impenetrable fog. Elizabeth's body grew limp, and she sank to her knees, her world spiralling into darkness. She fought against the encroaching unconsciousness, desperately grasping at fragments of reality slipping through her fingertips.

As Elizabeth's consciousness wavered on the edge of darkness, she became vaguely aware of multiple figures emerging from the shadows. Clad in sleek black attire, they encircled her with a precision that spoke of careful planning and impeccable execution. Her eyes struggled to focus, but she could make out the distinct outline of their imposing forms.

They stood like sentinels, an army of David Scarlett's men, a force that seemed to materialize out of thin air. Each one exuded an air of silent determination, their features hidden beneath the shadows of their hoods. Elizabeth's heart pounded in her chest, a mix of fear and anticipation coursing through her veins.

As the figures closed in, their movements synchronised with a calculated choreography. They formed a ring around her, a living barrier that reinforced her isolation. She was trapped, a captive in the centre of this enigmatic web.

The weight of their presence bore down on her, an unspoken threat lingering in the air. Elizabeth's mind raced, her instincts urging her to fight, to escape the clutches of this unexpected entrapment. But her body remained unresponsive, paralyzed by the drug's hold.

She scanned the faces of the shadowy figures, searching for any sign of recognition or empathy. But their expressions were concealed, their intentions shrouded in mystery. Her gaze met one pair of eyes, cold and unyielding, staring back at her with an intensity that sent shivers down her spine. It was David Scarlett, the man who had once been her elusive quarry, now seemingly orchestrating this intricate charade.

The figures in black remained a haunting presence in her fading awareness, their enigmatic faces etched into her memory. The world faded away, and Elizabeth surrendered to the unconsciousness that enveloped her, her fate hanging precariously in the balance. But deep within her, a spark of resilience remained, ready to ignite into a blazing fire as she embarked on a journey to confront the shadows that lurked in the depths of her father's past.

CHAPTER NINE: THE SHADOW ORDER

Elizabeth slowly opened her eyes, greeted by the bright, sterile light that illuminated the room. As her vision adjusted, she took in her surroundings, finding herself in a chamber lined with pristine white tiles. The walls rose up, forming an enclosed space that felt both confining and impersonal.

The room was devoid of any adornment or decoration, leaving it with an air of clinical minimalism. The white tiles that covered the walls, floor, and ceiling reflected the light, creating a stark, almost blinding effect. The surfaces were flawlessly smooth, devoid of any imperfections or blemishes, giving the room an eerie perfection.

As Elizabeth sat up on the soft white bed she had been lying on, she could feel the coolness of the tiles beneath her bare feet. The temperature in the chamber was carefully regulated, neither too hot nor too cold, contributing to the sterile ambience that permeated the space.

The room seemed to stretch out in all directions, creating a sense of infinite space. There were no windows or visible doors, making it appear as if the chamber was an isolated pocket within a larger labyrinthine structure. Elizabeth couldn't shake off the feeling of being trapped, contained within these walls.

Her gaze travelled across the room, searching for any signs of life or clues about her current predicament. The ceiling was equipped with recessed, bright lights that cast a harsh glow, illuminating every corner of the chamber. The light, though necessary, seemed invasive, almost oppressive, intensifying the sterile atmosphere.

There were no visible cameras or surveillance equipment, but Elizabeth couldn't shake off the sense of being watched. She felt as if unseen eyes were monitoring her every move, heightening her anxiety and wariness.

The room lacked furniture or personal belongings, leaving it bare and utilitarian. It seemed designed for function rather than comfort, a place meant for containment and control. The absence of any personal touches added to the disconcerting feeling that she was nothing more than a pawn in a much larger game.

The silence within the chamber was profound. The absence of any sound, apart from the soft hum of unseen machinery, added to the eerie ambience. The hush seemed to amplify the sound of her own breathing, creating an unsettling self-awareness.

As Elizabeth stood up from the bed, her gaze travelled once more across the chamber. Her eyes came to rest on a seemingly impenetrable wall where she expected to find a door. To her surprise, what she discovered instead was a large framed window that stretched across one side of the chamber. Through the transparent barrier, she caught a glimpse of the outside world, revealing a scene that sent chills down her spine.

The window offered a view into an expansive room with guards dressed in black. Their presence was imposing, their figures shrouded in secrecy. They stood tall and vigilant, their eyes hidden behind tinted goggles, creating an air of intimidation.

Elizabeth's gaze shifted from one guard to another, noting the precision with which they patrolled the area. Their movements were calculated, each step purposeful, as if rehearsed countless times.

The room was stark and barren, devoid of any signs of life or vegetation. Its cold, concrete ground seemed to reflect the solemnity and seriousness of the situation. The atmosphere outside was cloaked in an eerie stillness, as if time itself had frozen, leaving only a sense of impending danger hanging in the air.

Elizabeth caught glimpses of other structures in the room, their purpose shrouded in mystery. Darkened hallways, obscured doorways, and shadowy corners beckoned her curiosity, whispering secrets she was determined to uncover. The architecture hinted at hidden passageways and concealed chambers, where untold truths might lie in wait.

As she continued to observe, her eyes met those of one of the guards. Even from behind the tinted goggles, she could sense the intensity of their gaze, a silent warning not to venture further. The guard's stance was rigid, their presence a reminder of the formidable obstacle that stood between her and freedom.

Her eyes shifted back to the window, contemplating the risk of attempting an escape. Seeing there was no way out, she screamed out to the guards

'Where is David Scarlett?'

And Elizabeth's desperate cry echoed through the chamber, but the guards stationed outside the window remained unmoved, their stoic expressions unyielding. It was as if her words had been swallowed by the vast expanse of the room, disappearing into the air without making a sound. Frustration welled up inside her, threatening to overwhelm her senses.

She continued to call out, her voice growing hoarse with each plea. But the guards maintained their unwavering vigilance, their eyes fixed straight ahead as if they were deaf to her cries. It was a maddening silence, an impenetrable barrier that further heightened her sense of isolation.

Elizabeth's frustration soon turned into resignation, and she slid down to the cold, tiled floor. The weight of her helplessness bore down on her, crushing her spirit.

As she sat there, her back pressed against the unforgiving surface, Elizabeth's mind began to race with questions. Why had he not killed her at that moment? And what would he do with her now that he had her?

The absence of answers only fueled her frustration. The silence of the guards and the unyielding nature of her surroundings seemed to mock her. She closed her eyes and awaited the unknown.

Elizabeth drifted off and after what seemed like an hour, she woke up to the sound of a door of her confinement being opened. Elizabeth quickly stood up and she stood face to face with David Scarlett. He stood at the door alongside a company of guards, some of whom held a table and chair and walked in.

As David Scarlett, entered the chamber accompanied by his guards, the atmosphere grew tense with anticipation. Elizabeth's gaze locked onto his figure, her eyes scrutinizing every detail of his demeanour. His movements had an air of authority that commanded attention to them. David

Scarlett also had a tray in his hands, which had a kettle and a teacup on it.

The guards swiftly set up a table and chair, positioning them opposite each other. With meticulous precision, David Scarlett arranged the tray with a kettle and a cup of tea, ensuring every detail was in place. The sound of porcelain clinking against the surface filled the room, punctuating the silence that had settled between Elizabeth and him.

David Scarlett took his seat with measured composure. His gaze met Elizabeth's, his eyes exuding a mixture of curiosity and scrutiny. He exuded a commanding presence, his posture erect and his features exhibiting an air of self-assurance. It was clear that he was a man who had experienced so much accustomed to wielding power and authority.

Without a word, he reached for the kettle and poured the steaming liquid into the cup. The aroma of the tea filled the air, mingling with the tension that hung palpably in the chamber. With a deliberate motion, he pushed the cup towards Elizabeth.

The silence between them grew heavy, pregnant with unspoken questions and uncharted territory. Elizabeth's mind raced, attempting to decipher the intentions behind this unexpected encounter. Was it a move of respite? Or was it a calculated move, a psychological chess game designed to unravel her resolve?

She studied David Scarlett's face, searching for any flicker of emotion or insight. But his expression remained inscrutable, his features a mask of enigma. It seems he had mastered the art of concealing his true intentions, leaving Elizabeth to navigate the treacherous waters of uncertainty.

As Elizabeth contemplated the tea cup before her, she felt a mixture of trepidation and curiosity. The cup held the potential for both sustenance and poison. Yet, despite the ambiguity of the situation, Elizabeth found herself drawn to the cup. She was thirsty and required some substance in her system. Besides, the scent of the tea was glorious. Despite the tension in the room, it left some pleasantness in the air between David and Elizabeth.

David Scarlett broke the silence, his voice resonating with a quiet intensity.

"The tea will help with the sterilisers, Elizabeth. Have some"

As David Scarlett spoke, his voice held a tone of concern that Elizabeth hadn't expected. The mention of rest and healing tea caught her off guard, momentarily diverting her attention from the larger mysteries that loomed over them.

Elizabeth reached for the cup. Her hands were steadier this time. She brought it to her lips, the fragrant steam wafting towards her face, carrying a sense of comfort and rejuvenation. The liquid touched her tongue, releasing a burst of flavours that mingled harmoniously, soothing her parched throat.

David Scarlett's gaze never wavered as Elizabeth brought the cup to her lips.

The liquid caressed her palate, its familiar flavour offering a brief respite from the turmoil that engulfed her. The act of sipping the tea became a moment of silent communion, a shared experience that transcended words and boundaries.

As the tea trickled down her throat, Elizabeth felt a gentle warmth spread throughout her body. It was as if the liquid contained not only healing properties but also revitalising energy. She could almost imagine it coursing through her veins, restoring her vitality and strength.

With each sip, the fatigue and disorientation she had experienced began to dissipate. Her mind cleared, and a renewed sense of clarity emerged. The fog of confusion lifted, allowing her to see beyond the confines of the chamber and into the tangled web of secrets and lies that surrounded her.

The healing tea worked its magic, not only on a physical level but also on an emotional one. It was as if the warmth it infused within her awakened a dormant resolve. The fear that had gripped her moments ago began to recede, replaced by a newfound sense of purpose.

Elizabeth set the cup back on the table, her gaze meeting David Scarlett's once again. The silence that enveloped them seemed to stretch on indefinitely, each second laden with unspoken significance. It was as if the entire world had faded away, leaving only the two of them locked in an unyielding gaze.

David Scarlett's eyes returned to the tea in front of him. He reached his hands and sipped from his own cup of tea, a hint of admiration flickered in his eyes. Elizabeth remained silent, her gaze locked on his face, her heart pounding with anticipation.

"I must admit, Elizabeth," David began. He spoke with a measured tone, his words carrying a mix of acknowledgement and respect. "I have been observing your efforts closely. Your determination to unravel the truth about me is commendable. Your tenacity is unlike anything I've seen in a long while."

The weight of his words hung in the air, punctuated by the soft clinking of porcelain against porcelain. Elizabeth absorbed his words, her mind racing to make sense of this unexpected acknowledgement.

He continued, his voice tinged with a hint of nostalgia, "Your father... He was a remarkable man. A man who was ready to stand against those he worshipped because he wanted justice. He would be proud of the legacy you carry on. He would be proud of the relentless pursuit of truth that guides your actions."

Silence settled once more, as Elizabeth absorbed the weight of his words. She observed David carefully, searching for any sign of deception or ulterior motives. But his face remained impassive, his gaze steady, as if he were sincerely acknowledging her achievements.

As David finished his tea, he placed the cup gently back on the table. Their gazes locked, and Elizabeth could sense the unspoken understanding between them. With a faint smile, David rose from his chair, his posture commanding, yet there was an air of vulnerability about him. It was as if he carried the weight of a thousand secrets, but also a glimmer of hope for resolution.

"I appreciate your efforts, Elizabeth," he said, his voice filled with a mix of gratitude and caution. "But there are matters at play beyond your individual pursuit.'

David Scarlett stopped pacing and looked at Elizabeth, there was a glint in her eyes, yet his face remained stoic. 'I'm aware your findings have trailed me to be a suspect in her father's death. I'm sure you already know my relationship with your dad, and the things we achieved together. I would never do such to him' David Scarlett said, assuring Elizabeth

David Scarlett's words hung in the air, their weight pressing against the walls of the chamber. Elizabeth listened intently, her eyes fixed on him, searching for any trace of deception or sincerity.

He continued, his voice tinged with a hint of nostalgia and remorse. "Your father and I had a unique relationship. We were not the best of friends. But we stood for the same principles and fought for it. We achieved great things, things that were meant to bring about positive change in this world. I could never betray him, Elizabeth."

Elizabeth's mind raced, her thoughts colliding in a whirlwind of conflicting emotions. She had spent countless hours piecing together the fragments of her father's life, and the more she discovered, the more enigmatic the truth became. Could David Scarlett truly be innocent? Could their relationship have been as profound as he claimed?

'And since I know it would be easy for you to believe me. I could provide evidence of those who were involved.' David Scarlett said, resuming his pacing.

Elizabeth's eyes widened in anticipation as David Scarlett made his unexpected offer. The possibility of concrete evidence, of unveiling the hidden truths and exposing those responsible, ignited a flicker of hope within her. She had spent countless hours sifting through fragments, chasing shadows, and now the prospect of a breakthrough seemed within reach.

Still, she couldn't help but be confused by who this man was. This confusion morphed into a strong irritation.

'Who are you?! Who is David Scarlett?' Elizabeth's voice cut through the air, filled with a mix of frustration and desperation. The weight of uncertainty, the countless theories and speculations that had haunted her for years, now converged upon this enigmatic figure before her. David Scarlett, the man who had eluded her grasp, now seemed elusive in a different way—his very existence questioned.

Her gaze bore into him, searching for answers within his eyes. The silence stretched, heavy with anticipation

David stopped his pacing to look back at Elizabeth, somewhat taken aback by this question.

David Scarlett's chuckle filled the room, breaking the tension that had settled between them. Elizabeth couldn't help but feel a mix of confusion and frustration at his response. She had hoped for clarity, for a direct answer to the questions that had haunted her for so long. Yet, it seemed that David's enigmatic nature would persist.

As the echoes of his laughter faded away, a heavy silence settled upon the room. It was an eerie stillness, punctuated only by the soft hum of the ventilation system and the distant sound of footsteps echoing in the corridor beyond. Elizabeth's gaze remained fixed on David, her eyes searching his face for any sign of vulnerability or hidden agendas.

'Well, those are two widely different questions? Answering that will keep us here all day long,' He finally said meeting Elizabeth's gaze.

The silence in the room resumed. Minutes stretched into what felt like an eternity as the weight of their unspoken words hung in the air. It was as if the room itself held its breath, captivated by the uncertainty that swirled between them. Elizabeth's mind raced, a whirlwind of thoughts and emotions colliding within her.

Elizabeth's gaze remained locked with David's, a silent exchange of unspoken thoughts and emotions. The silence seemed to amplify the tension, intensifying Elizabeth's demand for the truth. She yearned for a resolution, for a breakthrough that would bring clarity and the truth she so desperately sought. Her eyes remained locked with David Scarlett in her stare down.

David Scarlett shifted his gaze from Elizabeth and sighed, melting off the tension that stood between them.

'Who am I? I am Daniel Carter, but my mission is David Scarlett...' Daniel Carter started his story with its origins in Germany, after the Second World War. To when he was arrested and released.

'This was when David Scarlett's mission began. The notion of a revenge mission, a quest to expose the truth and bring justice to those who had unjustly imprisoned me for years.'

Elizabeth leaned forward, her curiosity piqued by Daniel's revelation.

'As I delved deeper into my quest for justice, and succeeded', Daniel continued, 'I realised that my own suffering was just a small part of a larger problem. Oppressive governments and corrupt regimes were inflicting injustices on countless individuals, suppressing the truth and silencing those who dared to challenge their power."

Daniel walked to his chair and carefully leaned on it, his voice steady. "I decided to use my skills and resources to form a network of like-minded individuals, each seeking justice in their own corners of the world. Together, we strive to uncover the truth, expose corruption, and provide support to those who have been oppressed. We became David Scarlett."

Elizabeth absorbed his words, her mind racing with the implications of his network.

A small smile played on David's lips as he spoke, tinged with a mix of pride and caution. "David Scarlett is a delicate dance, Elizabeth. We operate with utmost discretion and employ a variety of strategies. Our network spans different sectors—journalists, human rights advocates, hackers, and more. We collaborate, share information, and support each other's efforts, always mindful of the risks involved."

He paused for a moment, his gaze piercing into Elizabeth's. "I have to admit, our work is dangerous. We've encountered obstacles, faced threats, and seen the consequences of challenging the status quo. Yet, the pursuit of justice compels us forward, driving us to expose the truth and protect the vulnerable."

'You mean challenging the status quo by numerous criminal activities?' Elizabeth interjected. Her voice was filled with scepticism as she interrupted,

Daniel shook his head, his expression grave. "No, Elizabeth. It is true that our actions may be seen as unconventional and operate outside the bounds of traditional systems. But we do not engage in criminal activities for personal gain or chaos. David Scarlett exposes the truth and holds those in power accountable."

He moved up to his chair, settled down, and leaned forward to Elizabeth, his eyes earnest. "You have to understand, Elizabeth, the intelligence community and those who wield power often paint us as criminals because our methods challenge their authority and disrupt their carefully constructed narratives. The infiltrators in the system have distorted our image, manipulating the truth to protect their positions of power."

Elizabeth absorbed his words, the gravity of the situation sinking in. The notion that those in power could manipulate the narrative to vilify those seeking justice sent a chill down her spine. She had always suspected this, but now Daniel mentioned it, it suddenly became clear to her.

Daniel leaned back in his chair, his gaze focused and intense. "Let me ask you this, Elizabeth: why is the intelligence community so obsessed with David Scarlett, the perceived 'criminal,' instead of focusing on the real threats that endanger our very existence?'

He paused, allowing his words to sink in. "You see, the intelligence community is fixated on maintaining the status quo, protecting their own interests, and preserving the established power structures. They have become complacent, prioritizing their own narratives and self-preservation over the greater good."

His voice carried a mix of frustration and determination. "Meanwhile, there are real threats lurking in the shadows, like the Shadow Order, the Russian agency that intends the turn the West nuke against them'

'Shadow Order?' Elizabeth leaned forward in curiosity. 'Is that what they are called?'

Daniel nodded steadily. 'These people possess the knowledge and capability to wreak havoc on our society. Yet, the intelligence community, blinded by their own preconceived notions and fear of disruption, turns a blind eye."

Elizabeth's mind raced, connecting the dots and seeing the larger picture unfold. The complexity of the world she had stepped into grew more intricate with every revelation. She realized that the battle for truth and justice was not simply black and white, but a myriad of shades of grey.

Her mind swirled with a multitude of questions as she contemplated the revelations Daniel had shared. She couldn't help but feel a mixture of curiosity, apprehension, and a deep longing for answers.

Sitting in the sterile chamber, Elizabeth felt a surge of frustration and determination welling up within her. She needed to uncover the truth, to piece together the fragments of her father's life and the secrets he had been entangled in. She wanted to understand the extent of Daniel's network and the risks involved in becoming a part of it. But most importantly, she yearned to find closure and justice for her father's untimely demise.

As she observed Daniel, sitting calmly across from her, she noticed the flicker of sadness in his eyes, as if he carried the weight of countless stories and untold truths. The silence between them stretched, heavy with unspoken words and unanswered questions.

'I recall that moment in the cell, after several years had passed and I had hoped for death. I stood up and looked at myself in the mirror. I knew that moment death was never going to come till I finished what I was meant to finish years ago.'

Elizabeth listened intently, her heart felt soaked with heaviness as the weight of his words settled on her.

As Daniel spoke, there was a flicker of emotions in her eyes. 'Unfortunately,' he continued, 'I couldn't get everyone. I had not gained enough power. I was gone past my prime and my strength was not as they were before. I couldn't save your dad from these people.'

Elizabeth's heart sank as Daniel's words hung heavy in the air. A mixture of disappointment and sorrow washed over her, realising that her father's fate had been sealed long before Daniel's journey began.

A profound sense of grief enveloped her as she imagined her father's struggles, the battles he fought alone, and the ultimate price he had paid. She couldn't help but feel a pang of regret, questioning whether there had been a missed opportunity, a chance to save him from the clutches of those who sought to silence him.

Her mind raced with conflicting emotions—admiration for Daniel's tenacity, gratitude for his honesty, but also a lingering sense of sadness for the things that could never be undone. The weight of the truth settled upon her shoulders, stirring up anger and impatience within her

'Who killed my dad?!' Elizabeth roared out, her voice filled with desperation.

Elizabeth's impatience and frustration boiled over, and she couldn't contain her urgent need for answers any longer.

Daniel, taken aback by the raw intensity of Elizabeth's outburst, paused for a moment, allowing her words to resonate. His gaze softened, revealing a mixture of empathy and contemplation.

As he stared into the depths of Elizabeth's eyes, Daniel's expression turned contemplative, his brows furrowing slightly. He weighed his words carefully, aware of the magnitude they held. The search for truth, justice, and redemption had been his driving force, and he was determined to provide Elizabeth with whatever clarity he could offer.

"Reinhardt," Daniel began, his tone tinged with a mix of frustration and empathy "is a master manipulator, a puppeteer pulling the strings from the shadows. He had once been part of an intricate web of covert operations, one in which I was a part of earlier in life. After your father and I revealed the

Soviet Union's infiltrators in the system, he escaped, allowing him to regroup and solidify his position in the world of espionage."

'Reinhardt was apprehended before he could get any further with his agenda. He agreed to work as a double agent so as not to be killed but he had his hidden agenda in the process.'

"The demise of the Soviet Union left a power vacuum in the world of intelligence," Daniel continued, his voice tinged with a heavy sigh. "Reinhardt, ever the opportunist, saw this as his chance to rise from the ashes and build an empire of his own. He returned to the organisation that had once utilised his services. With his vast knowledge of espionage techniques and access to sensitive information, Reinhardt set out to rebuild the very organisation that had once employed him. But this time, he had grander ambitions."

Elizabeth listened intently, her eyes focused on Daniel as he continued to unravel the complex web of intrigue surrounding Reinhardt. She couldn't help but feel a mixture of apprehension and curiosity, her mind racing with questions about the extent of Reinhardt's power and influence.

"As he returned to Russia," Daniel explained, "Reinhardt formed alliances with influential individuals within the intelligence community, both domestically and abroad. Together, they sought to create a formidable network that could manipulate global affairs to their advantage."

Daniel's eyes narrowed, his gaze steady as he spoke. "Reinhardt's ambitions extend far beyond personal gain. He harbours a dangerous ideology, a belief in reshaping the world order according to his twisted vision. His actions are not driven by mere greed or power but by a fervent desire to manipulate the very fabric of society."

Daniel continued, his eyes clouded with a mix of anger and frustration. "Reinhardt leveraged his knowledge and connections while serving as a double agent to leak sensitive secrets of the West to the Russian espionage organisation. These leaks, like poison seeping into the veins of the Western intelligence apparatus, gave rise to a new wave of infiltrations and data theft."

Elizabeth's brow furrowed.

Daniel's voice took on a sombre tone as he continued, "Reinhardt's actions have allowed the Shadow Order, Russian espionage organisation, to gain significant power and influence. They have infiltrated governments, corporations, and key institutions, sowing seeds of discord and manipulating events to further their own agenda."

Daniel's voice filled the room, recounting the tragic events that had unfolded. "Reinhardt's plan to infiltrate London was met with a formidable obstacle from Mason," he began. "Your father had an unwavering dedication to his work and a strong commitment to protecting the integrity of the city. This became a thorn in Reinhardt's side. To Reinhardt, Mason needed to be taken out"

Elizabeth listened intently, her heart heavy with grief and anger.

Daniel's voice grew sombre as he continued, "In his bid to eliminate Mason, Reinhardt had to be cautious. He couldn't afford for this assassination to be traced back to him or his shadowy Russian organization. A direct link would unravel the carefully constructed web of deception he had woven.

You see, Reinhardt is known for killing his victims using the Ricin poison. Instead of employing his notorious weapon of choice, he opted for a more covert method. It was a choice designed to mask his involvement and confuse investigators.'

"The order was given to Reinhardt's men," Daniel explained, his voice tinged with bitterness. "They were instructed to carry out the assassination swiftly and silently, leaving no evidence behind that could be linked back to Reinhardt or his organisation.'

Elizabeth's eyes welled with tears as the weight of her father's untimely demise settled upon her. The knowledge that he had been caught in the crossfire of a power struggle, his life cut short by forces beyond his control, was almost too much to bear. She clenched her fists as her grief transformed into a burning desire for vengeance.

Daniel continued, his voice trembling slightly. "Reinhardt's organisation grew in strength and influence and he soon found himself entangled in a web of political complexities. The very organisation he had built with his cunning and ruthlessness began to see him as expendable, a mere pawn in their larger game."

'The higher-ups within Reinhardt's organisation, driven by their own sinister agendas, saw him as a liability. They perceived him as a potential political threat to their own power and control. And so, they made a chilling decision: to eliminate Reinhardt."

A heavy silence settled in the room as the gravity of the situation sank in.

"And how did they eliminate him?" Elizabeth finally asked, her voice filled with a mix of anger and unease.

Daniel's eyes met Elizabeth's, his gaze steady and resolute. "They used Reinhardt's own weapon against him," he replied, his voice tinged with irony. "The deadly poison, ricin, which he had employed countless times to dispose of his targets, became the tool of his demise."

Elizabeth sat in stunned silence, her mind swirling with a mix of emotions. The weight of Daniel's words hung heavy in the air. The irony of Reinhardt's demise was both poetic and chilling.

Closing her eyes, Elizabeth took a deep breath, allowing the weight of the revelation to wash over her. The conflicting emotions of anger, unease and relief battled within her. The man who had orchestrated her father's murder had met his own sinister fate, a victim of the very system he had manipulated so expertly.

A rush of memories flooded her mind—the sound of her father's laughter, his guiding presence, and the warmth of his love. The pain of his loss resurfaced, intensifying her determination to bring justice to his memory.

'It's not over, Elizabeth.' Daniels' voice resumed "The strength and influence of Reinhardt's organisation continued to grow. They call themselves the Shadow Order, casting a dark shadow over the world", he explained. "To stop them, I found myself embroiled in operations across the globe. Our goal was to disrupt their plans, gather intelligence, and expose their network."

Elizabeth opened her eyes and listened to Daniel

"The intelligence community has often found it difficult to distinguish between the actions of the Shadow order and David Scarlett", Daniel continued. "This is because anywhere they go, we go and to defeat them. And most of the time, the intelligence community draws us out as the scapegoat.'

Daniel's voice took on a tone of defiance as he continued, "I can't blame them for such actions. There are already numerous infiltrators in the system, diverting the intelligence community force from the truth. But we know the truth. We know the extent of Reinhardt's malevolence and the need to expose his organisation's crimes. We worked tirelessly to gather evidence, connect the dots, and shed light on their operations, even in the face of constant confusion and misdirection."

Daniel leaned forward in his chair, his gaze focused and intense "Elizabeth," he began, "this Russian organisation is unlike any other. They are led by extremists and psychopaths who have an insatiable hunger for power and control, especially over the West."

Elizabeth's eyes widened as she absorbed his words. The gravity of the situation became increasingly apparent to her. She had been unwittingly entangled in a dangerous web, pitted against a formidable enemy driven by sinister motives.

"These individuals will stop at nothing to achieve their objectives," Daniel continued, his voice filled with conviction. "They employ ruthless tactics and train only the most menacing and cold-blooded individuals. These men are adept at manipulation, espionage, and violence, willing to sacrifice anyone and anything to further their cause."

Elizabeth listened intently, her mind racing to comprehend the magnitude of the threat they were up against.

"Reinhardt's organization operates in the shadows, unseen and undetected by most," Daniel explained, his voice tinged with a mix of frustration and determination. "They infiltrate governments, corporations, and influential circles, amassing wealth and power, and exploiting vulnerabilities for their own gain. Their reach extends far and wide, making it difficult to distinguish friend from foe."

Elizabeth felt a knot forming in her stomach as the reality of the situation sank in.

"These psychopaths view the West as their ultimate prize," Daniel continued, his voice laced with a mix of concern and urgency. "They seek to destabilize governments, sow discord, and exploit divisions within societies. Their ultimate goal is to seize power and control, leaving chaos and devastation in their wake."

Elizabeth's mind raced with the enormity of the situation. The knowledge that a group of ruthless extremists had the power to manipulate world events and jeopardise countless lives was both alarming and infuriating.

'I carry the weight of firsthand experience and a deep understanding of the Russian organisation's inner workings because of the years spent combating their operations. I have sharpened insight. And their actions only fuel my resolve to bring them down!'

'We will bring them down!' Elizabeth rose up to her feet with anger and a renewed sense of purpose. This was no longer just a mission for glory for her. She realised that her pursuit of truth and justice was personal. It is about avenging her father's death and it is about safeguarding the principles of freedom and democracy that were under threat. She knew she couldn't do it alone, but with Daniel's guidance and their collective determination, they had a fighting chance.

CHAPTER TEN: THE FINAL CONFRONTATION

The next day, Elizabeth stood in her apartment, her eyes fixed on the mirror as she adjusted her dark suit. Today, she had chosen a more professional and commanding attire, opting for a tailored suit with trousers. As she fastened the buttons, her mind was focused on the task ahead.

Her apartment, once a place of solace and refuge, now felt like a temporary respite amidst the storm that awaited her outside. The walls seemed to echo with her determination, each step she took was a testament to her unwavering commitment to seek justice and avenge her father's death.

As she glanced at the clock, the hands ticking steadily towards the appointed hour, a mix of anticipation and nerves fluttered in her stomach. The weight of the responsibility she had willingly taken on settled upon her shoulders, reminding her of the dangers that lay ahead.

But Elizabeth was undeterred. She had spent countless days with Daniel, planning, and connecting the dots, gathering the necessary evidence to expose the Russian organisation's intricate web of deceit. The information she had obtained, the names and faces of those involved, fueled her desire to dismantle their operation and ensure they faced the consequences of their actions.

However, she knew she could not do it alone. So Elizabeth approached Emily and Hugh, her closest allies in the pursuit of truth and justice, seeking their assistance in the perilous task ahead. Their combined skills and resources would be invaluable in their fight against this formidable enemy.

Emily initially resisted the idea. She was well aware of the dangers involved and was not ready for this out-of-status quo mission. Doubt clouded her eyes as she contemplated the risks they would be undertaking.

But Elizabeth, driven by her unwavering determination, knew that she needed to convince Emily of the significance of their mission. She saw the flicker of curiosity and interest in her eyes and knew that she could exploit that to sway her decision.

They came to her truce. Emily would have led on the David Scarlett case, and Elizabeth would step down for her. She highlighted the connection between the Russian organisation and the events surrounding David Scarlett's mysterious operations. She painted a picture of the web of corruption and deceit that spanned continents, leaving no room for doubt that their involvement was not only necessary but vital.

Emily's scepticism wavered as the allure of uncovering the truth beckoned her. The prospect of shedding light on the enigma that had haunted them for so long proved too tempting to resist. The chance to bring closure to the unresolved case of David

Scarlett, a man whose fate had remained shrouded in mystery, was an opportunity that Emily couldn't ignore.

Hugh, on the other hand, was ever the steadfast and loyal ally. He had been drawn into the mission long before Elizabeth sought his help. He had also been captivated by the harrowing tale of Elizabeth's father and the revelations surrounding the Russian organisation's nefarious activities. The magnitude of the threat they posed to the West had struck a chord deep within him, fueling his determination to make a difference.

As Elizabeth shared the detailed account of what had transpired and the depth of the conspiracy they were facing, Hugh's surprise was palpable. The weight of the information hit him like a tidal wave, shaking him to his core. The realization that Elizabeth's father had been caught in the crossfire, a casualty of a much larger scheme, only fueled his resolve to seek justice and protect the innocent.

Already convinced of the imminent danger that the Russian organization posed, Hugh had begun his own investigations and gathering evidence. He understood the gravity of the situation, and his unwavering belief in the power of truth and the necessity of taking action pushed him to be one step ahead.

With his determination already aligned with Elizabeth's, Hugh welcomed her request for assistance with open arms.

As the plan began to take shape, Elizabeth, Emily, and Hugh understood the critical role they each had to play.

Their objective was clear: They were to infiltrate a secret meeting between state officials and the Russian spy organisation in South Africa, where the final code granting access to the nuclear weapon facilities in the West would be exchanged. It was a pivotal moment, one that could decide the fate of nations and the safety of millions.

David Scarlett's men, skilled and battle-tested, would be ready to ambush the meeting and prevent the Russian organization from obtaining the code. However, they needed insiders to acquire the files before the exchange took place. Elizabeth and Emily agreed to masquerade as escorts, using their cunning and resourcefulness to retrieve the vital information.

Meanwhile, Hugh, equipped with his extensive knowledge of intelligence operations, worked closely with David Scarlett's men. He shared crucial information about the layout of the meeting venue, the expected attendees, and the security measures in place. His presence would not only bolster the raid but also enable immediate communication with the intelligence community, ensuring swift dissemination of vital intelligence.

Elizabeth Morgan stood before the mirror, her gaze fixated on her reflection. Her eyes sparkled with determination and her features exuded a resolute strength. She had spent hours preparing for this moment, mentally and physically, knowing that the mission ahead demanded her unwavering focus and resolve.

Her dark suit, tailored to perfection, accentuated her poised demeanour. She adjusted the collar, straightened her tie, and ensured that every detail was in place. This was no longer just a mission for glory or justice; it was personal. The memory of her father's death, the legacy he had left behind, and the imminent threat posed by the Russian organization fueled her determination.

She reached into a drawer and retrieved a small, compact gun. Carefully, she holstered it inside her suit, ensuring it was secure and easily accessible if the need arose.

As she stepped out of her apartment, the weight of her purpose hung heavy in the air. The world outside seemed to hold its breath, awaiting the unfolding of events that would shape the course of history. Elizabeth knew that she couldn't afford to falter or hesitate. She had to confront the darkness head-on, expose the truth, and protect the innocent from the clutches of the Russian organization.

Her path led her to the airport, with each step, Elizabeth's resolve deepened. She had come a long way since the inception of her mission, forging alliances, unravelling secrets, and enduring the trials that had tested her every limit. This journey had transformed her.

Under the cover of darkness, Elizabeth and Emily arrived in South Africa, the location of the highly anticipated meeting. Their plane touched down smoothly, the hum of the engines fading as the night air embraced them. They were now in the heart of Johannesburg, a city teeming with life, energy, and the promise of intrigue.

As they stepped off the plane, the cool African breeze whispered secrets of the night, carrying with it a sense of anticipation. The streets of Johannesburg were dimly lit, casting long shadows that seemed to dance alongside the women as they made their way through the city. Elizabeth and Emily moved with purpose, their steps measured and deliberate.

Their destination was a grand hall nestled in the heart of Johannesburg, where the meeting was set to take place. As they approached the venue, the faint sound of music drifted through the night, accompanied by the soft murmur of voices. The hall was a beacon of light, its ornate exterior and grandeur serving as a stark contrast to the secrecy and danger that lay within.

The entrance to the hall was guarded by imposing figures, their stern expressions a testament to the seriousness of the event. Elizabeth and Emily exchanged a knowing glance, understanding the importance of remaining inconspicuous. They were not just attendees of this lavish party; they were undercover agents, ready to unveil the hidden truths that lay behind the façade.

Dressed in elegant gowns that mirrored the sophistication of the occasion, Elizabeth and Emily approached the entrance with an air of confidence. The guards eyed them briefly, their scrutiny sharpened. With practised grace, the women presented their invitations, their identities hidden beneath the guise of high-class escorts.

Once inside, the hall unveiled its opulence, with chandeliers sparkling overhead and the room abuzz with the chatter of influential figures from around the world. The atmosphere crackled with tension and masked intentions, like a fragile web spun by those who sought power and control.

Elizabeth and Emily skillfully navigated through the crowd, their eyes scanning the room for any signs of familiarity or danger. They exchanged coded glances and subtle gestures, their connection unspoken yet palpable. This was the moment they had prepared for, the apex of their mission, and failure was not an option.

As they mingled with the guests, Elizabeth and Emily eavesdropped on conversations. They carefully observed the body language of attendees, searching for any hints of deception or hidden agendas.

The tension in the room escalated as the state officials from all over the world gathered. Whispers of political manoeuvres, clandestine alliances, and the impending danger that loomed over the West filled the air. Elizabeth and Emily remained alert, their senses attuned to every detail, as they aimed to intercept the files containing the final code before they fell into the wrong hands.

They stood together in the midst of the party, their eyes scanning the room with a keen sense of awareness. The air was thick with anticipation, as guests conversed in hushed tones, their voices intermingling with the melodic notes of the music playing softly in the background.

Suddenly, a group of white Russian individuals entered the hall, their presence commanding attention. Clad in dark tuxedos that exuded an air of formality, they moved with a certain aura of confidence and authority. Elizabeth's eyes widened as she recognized them from their previous encounters with Crane and Peter Bashir, their menacing looks etched in her memory.

She discreetly nudged Emily, directing her attention towards the group. Emily's gaze followed Elizabeth's gesture, and a flicker of recognition danced in her eyes. They knew that these individuals were key players in the Russian spy organisation they were seeking to expose.

As the group mingled with other guests, Elizabeth and Emily discreetly observed their interactions. They noted the subtle exchanges, the guarded conversations, and the occasional glances cast towards the more influential figures in the room.

Elizabeth and Emily exchanged a silent understanding. With practised grace, they moved closer to the group, positioning themselves strategically to eavesdrop on conversations while remaining inconspicuous.

The Russians spoke in coded terms with low voices, their words laced with an undercurrent of urgency. Emily's eyes darted between the Russians, her mind racing to decipher their intentions. She recognized the calculated manner in which they operated, their allegiance firmly rooted in power and control.

Elizabeth's heart pounded with a mix of determination and concern. With a quick glance at Emily, she subtly gestured for her to continue monitoring the Russians while she sought an opportunity to retrieve the files containing the final code.

Emily maintained her watchful gaze on the Russian group, analysing their every move. She detected a sense of restlessness, a subtle unease that hinted at their awareness that they could be watched. Their eyes darted nervously, scanning the room as if anticipating the presence of unforeseen threats.

Suddenly, Emily's attention was caught by a fleeting moment of vulnerability. One of the Russians momentarily excused himself from the group, his gaze fixated on a hidden corner of the hall. It was a brief window of opportunity that Emily couldn't afford to miss.

With her senses heightened and adrenaline coursing through her veins, Emily moved swiftly, subtly trailing the Russian as he made his way towards the secluded corner. She carefully avoided drawing attention to herself, maintaining a safe distance to avoid arousing suspicion.

Elizabeth's mind raced, searching for a way to create a distraction that would draw the officials away from the room. She knew that accessing the locked room was crucial to obtaining the information they needed. Taking a deep breath, she assessed her surroundings, scanning for any potential resources that could aid her in her mission.

Her eyes landed on a nearby tray of champagne flutes, waiting to be served to the guests. An idea sparked in her mind, and a mischievous smile played at the corners of her lips. With a swift and deliberate motion, she grabbed the tray and sauntered towards a group of guests engaged in animated conversation.

Using her wit and charm, she expertly manoeuvred through the crowd, subtly bumping into a guest, causing a few champagne flutes to tumble from the tray and shatter on the floor. The sound of breaking glass echoed through the room, capturing the attention of those nearby, especially the state officials and the Russians, who grew weary of the room and decided to leave.

While they left, Elizabeth overheard a state official nervously confessing to his acquaintance beside him that they had locked the files and codes in a secret room away from the Russians in case the Russians wanted to play foul like they are aware they usually do.

Elizabeth listened attentively to the room door number and exited quickly to the room. She got to the room door and realised the guards had been dispersed from their duty to attend to the state officials who were meeting with the Russians. Quickly she took off her escort dress, sneaked inside and quickly shut the door behind her.

Inside, she found herself surrounded by a dimly lit space, filled with files, documents, and high-tech surveillance equipment. She quickly assessed the room, her eyes scanning for any sign of the files containing the final code. It didn't take long for her to locate a secure safe hidden within a cabinet.

Taking a deep breath, Elizabeth reached into her pocket and retrieved a small lock-picking kit. With precision and skill, she began to work on the safe, her hands steady despite the adrenaline coursing through her veins. The task seemed to take an eternity, each click of the lock raising her anticipation.

Finally, the safe clicked open, revealing a stack of files neatly organized within. Elizabeth's heart raced as she searched through the documents, her eyes scanning for any indication of the final code. She knew that time was running out, and she needed to find the information before the Russian spy organization could execute their deadly plans.

And then, among the sea of papers, her eyes fell upon a file labelled "Project Epsilon." With trembling hands, she opened the file and found the document they had been searching for—the final code that would grant the Russian organisation unprecedented control over the nuclear weapon facilities.

A mixture of relief and determination washed over Elizabeth as she tucked the file securely into her suit. With a sense of urgency, she carefully closed the safe, leaving no trace of her presence. As she turned to exit the room, Elizabeth's heart skipped a beat as she turned around and found herself surrounded by the Russian agents. Their stern expressions and rapid-fire words in Russian conveyed a sense of danger that sent a chill down her spine. She realized that her cover might have been compromised, and panic threatened to overtake her.

Instinctively, Elizabeth's hand reached for the gun concealed within her suit, ready to defend herself if necessary. Her mind raced, searching for a way out of this precarious situation. The Russian agents laughed at her. 'You can take us out with that one stick in your hands.' one of them said with a menacing grin.

Elizabeth's instincts kicked into overdrive. With a swift decision, she switched gears, transitioning from a calm negotiator to a determined fighter.

Adrenaline surged through Elizabeth's veins as she swiftly assessed her surroundings, calculating her every move. She unleashed her full combat skills, unleashing a torrent of relentless strikes and evasive manoeuvres.

Her fists and legs moved with lightning speed, each strike calculated to disarm and incapacitate her opponents. Elizabeth's determination to protect the valuable file and ensure her survival fueled every move, turning her into a force to be reckoned with.

The Russian agents, initially caught off guard by Elizabeth's sudden transformation, soon regrouped and fought back with their own viciousness. It became a whirlwind of punches, kicks, and blocks as the room erupted into chaos. Furniture toppled, glasses shattered, and the sound of grunts and shouts filled the air.

Elizabeth's focus remained unwavering as she deftly navigated through the chaos. She anticipated her opponents' moves, evading their strikes with cat-like reflexes.

With each opponent she defeated, a surge of adrenaline coursed through Elizabeth's veins, fuelling her determination to emerge victorious. Her moves became more fluid and precise as if she had tapped into a wellspring of power that lay dormant within her.

As Elizabeth fought valiantly against the remaining Russian agents, the odds seemed to momentarily shift in her favour. She skillfully dodged blows and delivered powerful strikes, gradually gaining the upper hand. However, just as victory seemed within her grasp, a sudden turn of events shattered her momentum. Elizabeth brought out her gun to end things with her opponent now that most of them had been apprehended.

Out of nowhere, one of the Russian agents seized an opportune moment and managed to apprehend Elizabeth. With a swift and unexpected move, he disarmed her, knocking her gun out of her hand and sending her crashing to the ground. The room fell silent, the tension escalating as the agent loomed over her, weapon in hand.

Time seemed to slow down as Elizabeth's mind raced, assessing the dire situation she found herself in. The agent picked up the gun and pointed it at her. Fear threatened to grip her, but she drew upon her resilience and determination to stay focused.

Just as the agent prepared to pull the trigger, a burst of movement erupted from the corner of the room. Hug burst into the room, his presence catching the agent off guard. With a surge of strength and speed, he launched himself at the Russian, knocking him off balance.

The force of Hugh's impact sent both men tumbling to the ground, their bodies colliding with a thud. The agent's grip on the weapon loosened, and it skidded across the floor, momentarily forgotten. The room erupted into chaos once again as both men tumbled and punched each other.

Elizabeth quickly regained her footing, her eyes locked on her weapon that lay within reach. Instinct kicked in, and she lunged toward it, her fingers closing around the cold metal. With the gun firmly in her grasp, she pointed it at the fallen agent, her determination unwavering.

The agent, recovering from the surprise attack, attempted to regain control of the situation. He reached for his own weapon, his eyes filled with a mix of rage and desperation. But before he could retrieve it, Hugh, fueled by adrenaline and a sense of duty, swiftly rose to his feet and unleashed a series of powerful strikes upon the agent.

Blows landed with precision, each strike draining the agent's strength and resolve. Hugh's determination to protect Elizabeth and ensure the mission's success surged through him, intensifying his attacks. He fought with a controlled ferocity, unleashing a storm of punches and kicks that left the agent reeling.

Elizabeth, having regained her composure, joined the fray. With her gun in hand, she kept a steady aim on the agent, her finger poised on the trigger. She thought of her dad that moment and the three bullets shot into his heart. In a second, Elizabeth pulled the trigger into the agent's heart. Three loud and banging bullets into his heart.

Emily found herself facing a formidable opponent of her own. The Russian agent that left the party had the remaining code to infiltrate the West with him. Determined to retrieve the remaining code and protect her comrades, she focused all her energy on outmanoeuvring the Russian agent standing in her way.

Emily, too, was well-trained in combat and espionage. She possessed a quick mind and a keen sense of observation, which allowed her to identify weaknesses and exploit them. With a mixture of skill and resourcefulness, she launched a series of calculated strikes, hoping to subdue her adversary and retrieve the remaining code.

However, this particular Russian agent proved to be a formidable opponent. He countered Emily's moves with uncanny precision, effectively neutralizing her attacks and preventing her from gaining the upper hand. Despite her determination, Emily found herself overshadowed by the agent's superior strength and skill.

Realizing that she was overmatched, Emily made a split-second decision. She feigned vulnerability, momentarily lowering her guard to lure the agent into a false sense of security. The agent, believing he had gained the advantage, moved in closer, intending to apprehend Emily and secure his victory.

But just as he closed in, Emily unleashed a swift and unexpected manoeuvre. She executed a swift spin, using the agent's momentum against him. With a precise strike, she managed to disarm him, causing the code he held to go flying across the room. Emily's heart raced with a glimmer of hope as she realized she had momentarily gained the upper hand.

However, her victory was short-lived. The agent, fueled by his determination to protect the code and his organization's sinister plans, refused to give up. He lunged at Emily, overpowering her with sheer brute force. Despite her valiant efforts to defend herself, she found herself at the mercy of the agent and his reinforcements.

In an instant, Emily was surrounded by a group of Russian agents, her struggles futile against their combined strength. They quickly apprehended her, immobilizing her and taking control of the situation. Their menacing glares and cruel smiles conveyed their intentions clearly—

Emily's life hung in the balance, and they were not afraid to exploit that.

The Russian agents, now in control of the room, forced Emily to her knees, her hands bound and her spirit unbroken. They brought her before Hugh and Elizabeth, who stood with a mixture of concern and determination etched upon their faces. The agents, holding Emily captive, issued a chilling ultimatum—hand over the remaining code, or they would kill Emily.

The weight of the decision hung heavily in the air as Hugh and Elizabeth exchanged a knowing look. Their determination burned brighter than ever, but they also understood the gravity of the situation. The lives of their team members and the security of the Western world were at stake.

Elizabeth's mind raced, searching for a way out of this seemingly impossible predicament. She weighed the risks and consequences, considering every possible angle. She knew that the Russian agents would not hesitate to carry out their threats, but surrendering would mean their mission would fail, and the consequences could be catastrophic.

A few moments passed, and Elizabeth and Hugh exchanged a pained glance. With a resigned nod, Elizabeth and Hugh stepped forward, offering the files to the Russian agents. As they handed over the valuable information, a mixture of frustration and sorrow welled up within them.

The Russian agents, sensing victory, grinned triumphantly as they took possession of the files. They gloated, their menacing expressions mocking the defeat of their adversaries. As the Russian agents gloated over their apparent triumph, the room was filled with a heavy silence.

As the tension in the room reached its peak, a sudden, deafening noise reverberated through the air. The chandelier above swung and fell off the ceiling violently, and guests and agents alike looked up to the source of the commotion. To their astonishment, a helicopter descended from above, landing gracefully on the open roof of the grand hall.

The helicopter's blades sliced through the air with an ear-splitting roar, drowning out any attempt at communication. The gust of wind it created sent loose papers and debris flying through the room, adding to the chaos already unfolding. It was clear that this unexpected turn of events was carefully orchestrated by the Russian agents as a means of escape.

With precision and efficiency, the helicopter's doors slid open, revealing a group of heavily armed agents. Their dark uniforms and cold, calculating expressions left no doubt that they were prepared to do whatever it took to achieve their goals. The tension in the room thickened as they swiftly descended ropes, preparing to evacuate the area.

As Elizabeth, Hugh, and Emily prepared to confront these people, they realised the new arrivals were David Scarlett's men and the S.I.S (Secret Intelligence Service) agents.

With remarkable precision and agility, David Scarlett's men and the S.I.S team rappelled down onto the floor, their arrival causing a momentary halt in the chaos that engulfed the room.

The Russian agents, who moments ago believed they were on the brink of escaping with their ill-gotten files, found themselves caught off guard by this unforeseen development. The element of surprise now shifted in favour of Elizabeth, Hugh, Emily, and their newly arrived allies.

David Scarlett's men, renowned for their strategic brilliance and fearless determination, took charge of the situation. With a commanding presence, he coordinated his team, ensuring a seamless and synchronized operation. The S.I.S agents also moved swiftly and decisively, swiftly apprehending the stunned Russian agents before they could fully comprehend what was happening.

In a blur of coordinated movements, the S.I.S agents disarmed the Russian operatives, their training and skill evident in every calculated manoeuvre. With precise strikes and swift takedowns, they swiftly neutralized the threat posed by the Russian agents. The room became a battlefield, with the sounds of struggle and subdued grunts echoing through the grand hall.

The Russian agents, their arrogance shattered and their plans thwarted, lay defeated and apprehended on the floor. The weight of their crimes and their impending punishment hung heavy in the air. The guests who had once been captivated by the glamour of the occasion now watched in awe and relief, grateful for the intervention that had saved them from an unknown peril.

As the room began to regain a semblance of order, David Scarlett's men swiftly took control of the situation. They expertly secured the apprehended Russian agents, binding them tightly to ensure they posed no further threat. The S.I.S operatives, with their training honed to perfection, carried out the arrest with utmost professionalism and efficiency.

As Emily and Elizabeth caught sight of David Scarlett's men and the S.I.S agents joining forces with them, their initial shock quickly transformed into a mix of confusion and relief. The unexpected collaboration left them with questions swirling in their minds. However, before they could voice their concerns, Hugh stepped forward, ready to provide the much-needed explanation.

With a calm and composed demeanour, Hugh began to unveil the hidden layers of his plan. 'Behind the scenes, I had been in constant contact with the intelligence community, sharing critical information about the Russian agents and their nefarious activities. It had been my intention all along to ensure that they had sufficient evidence to prove David Scarlett's innocence and rally support from the S.I.S. for this operation.'

Hugh explained that the intelligence community had been closely monitoring the Russian agents' operation, tracing their movements, and gathering intelligence to dismantle their plans. When the opportunity arose to expose the true nature of the situation, Hugh had coordinated with the intelligence community to mobilize and provide support at the crucial moment.

Emily and Elizabeth listened intently, gradually piecing together the puzzle of Hugh's meticulous planning. The revelation brought a wave of relief, but also a sense of awe and admiration for Hugh's foresight and his ability to orchestrate such a complex operation.

As the dust settled, the S.I.S agents and David Scarlett maintained a watchful presence, their professionalism and expertise shining through. With the Russian agents apprehended and the files secured, they shifted their attention to debriefing and extracting any additional information that could help dismantle the spy network once and for all.

While Elizabeth, Emily and Hugh watched the fight they had planned meticulously for it to be over.

***

Emily and Elizabeth found themselves standing in the austere office of their superiors at the S.I.S headquarters, the next day. The air was heavy with anticipation as their superior's expressions reflected a mix of sternness and concern. The weight of their authority was palpable, and the atmosphere grew tense. The scolding continued, their voices firm and laced with disappointment.

'Elizabeth, your decision to go against established protocols and pursue a risky course of action was highly concerning. It compromised the integrity of the mission and put not only yourself but also the entire team at risk. We cannot stress enough the importance of following the procedures we have in place.' Agent Jacko banged against the table.

'I apologise, sir. In the heat of the moment, I believed it was the best course of action to protect the mission.' Elizabeth bowed slightly

He turned to Emily 'And you, Emily, you too made choices that deviated from our standard procedures. Your decision to follow Elizabeth without question was equally concerning. As a member of this agency, you have a responsibility to challenge and question actions that could potentially jeopardise the mission.'

Emily, whose eyes were settled on the floor, nodded slightly 'I understand, sir. I should have raised my concerns and evaluated the situation more thoroughly before acting.

'Your actions had the potential to compromise diplomatic relationships and the security of classified information. We cannot emphasize enough the importance of maintaining trust and upholding the agency's reputation. Your actions went against the established status quo.' Agent Tola said, calmly.

'We fully acknowledge the gravity of our actions, and we're prepared to face the consequences.' Emily said.

There was silence in the room for a moment. Agent Thon finally spoke, through his seemingly closed eyes. 'We recognize that your initiative and resourcefulness led to a significant breakthrough in neutralising the Russian spy network. Your audacity and commitment to the mission are commendable.'

'Indeed, your determination and courage did not go unnoticed. In light of the successful outcome of the mission, we have decided to promote both of you to higher ranks within the intelligence committee.' Agent Tola said with a smile across her face

Emily and Elizabeth looked at each other surprised

'This promotion comes with added responsibility. We expect you to channel your innovative thinking and resourcefulness within the framework of our established protocols. Learn from this experience, understand the consequences of your actions, and maintain a balance between taking risks and adhering to procedures.' Agent Thron said

'Your success should not overshadow the importance of following our guidelines. We trust that this incident has served as a valuable lesson and that you will continue to grow and develop as exceptional agents within the intelligence community.' Agent Tola said

Emily and Elizabeth nodded 'Thank you, sirs. We appreciate your guidance, and we will do our best to uphold the values and standards of this agency.

'That concludes our discussion. We have high expectations for both of you.

Go out there and make us proud. Dismissed.' Agent Tola said

With a mix of relief and determination, as Emily and Elizabeth left the room. As they stepped out of the meeting room, Emily couldn't help but wear a genuine smile on her face. She turned to Elizabeth, a glimmer of what looked like peace in her eyes.

'Elizabeth, I have something to tell you.' she turned to Elizabeth, who also stopped to look her Emily 'I've made a decision. I won't be accepting the promotion.'

Elizabeth looked at her with surprise and curiosity. 'What? Why?'

'I've realised something during this mission, Elizabeth. Life is precious, and there's so much more to experience outside the world of espionage. I want to live a life where I can explore and enjoy the simple pleasures without the constant complications and dangers that come with all these.'

Elizabeth's surprise turned into understanding, seeing the determination and serenity in Emily's eyes.

'I've been thinking about this for a while, and now feels like the right time. I want to embrace a new chapter of my life, filled with freedom and possibilities. I mean, I never thought I could be interested in children my whole life. But this moment. I think I'll love it too.'

Emily smiled warmly and placed a hand on Elizabeth's shoulder.

'I have no doubt that you'll find that balance, Elizabeth. You're a remarkable agent with a compassionate heart. Remember to take care of yourself along the way.'

Elizabeth nodded, a mix of determination and gratitude shining in her eyes.

'Thank you, Emily. Your friendship and support mean the world to me.'

As they walked together, a sense of renewal and liberation filled the air. With Emily embarking on her new adventures, and Elizabeth continuing her mission with renewed determination, fueled by the understanding that life is precious and meant to be cherished. That moment, Elizabeth remembered Hugh and ran out of the S.I.S headquarter to catch a taxi to the police station.

Elizabeth entered Hugh's office, finding him surrounded by a sea of files and an air of exhaustion hanging over him. She couldn't help but notice the weariness etched on his face. As their eyes met, a mixture of relief and joy washed over Hugh.

'Elizabeth' Hugh stood up to meet Elizabeth. 'I'm glad you're here.'

'I wanted to thank you, Hugh.' Elizabeth said, trying to catch her breath 'We wouldn't have been able to accomplish what we did without you.'

Hugh's expression softened, 'Thank you, Elizabeth. It was a risk I was willing to take.' his gaze shifted away from Elizabeth 'Sadly, my involvement has come at a cost. I've been demoted and have to step down from my position as the officer on duty.'

Elizabeth's face showed a mixture of surprise and concern.

'Hugh, I'm sorry to hear that. You didn't deserve this.'

Hugh sighed, his exhaustion evident in his voice. 'I understand the decision, Elizabeth. It's the consequence of me going against protocol and taking matters into my own hands. But don't worry about me. I'll find my way, and I'll continue to support the cause, even if it's from a different position.' he settled on his table, smiling at Elizabeth. His eyes softened as he gazed at Elizabeth.

"Elizabeth, there's something I need to tell you," Hugh said, his voice filled with a mixture of nervousness and determination. "Ever since we were young...I've... had these feelings for you. I know we started as friends. But over time, I think it has grown into something more."

Elizabeth listened intently, her own heart pounding in her chest. This was the moment she had waited for. The words she had waited for Hugh to say all these years.

He continued, his voice filled with sincerity, "There have been countless nights where I've dreamt of being with you, waking up wishing those dreams were reality. And now, in this moment, I can't keep it inside any longer. I'm in love with you, Elizabeth."

Elizabeth's breath caught in her throat, her mind racing to process the weight of Hugh's words. She had given up on the possibility of a romantic relationship with him long ago, but as he poured out his feelings, she realised the depth of their connection.

Touched by his honesty and bravery, Elizabeth reached out to Hugh and pulled him from the table. 'My dad says you don't tell a lady you love her while seated.' she chuckled at Hugh, who caught her gaze and smiled lightly.

Hugh's eyes searched hers, hopeful yet apprehensive. "I understand if this changes things between us, Elizabeth," he said, his voice filled with vulnerability. "But I couldn't keep this to myself any longer. I have to let you know how I feel."

Elizabeth's smile grew, her heartwarming at his words. She leaned in closer, closing the gap between them. "Hugh, you've been there for me through thick and thin, and your friendship has always been a source of strength. I can never imagine life without you."

Elizabeth leaned forward and pressed her lips against Hugh's lips. Their gentle kiss fuelled up a mix of excitement, and nervousness in them. The room grew warmer as their kiss intensified, and they held each other passionately.

As their lips parted, Elizabeth looked into Hugh's eyes, a newfound sense of joy and contentment settling within her. "I love you too, Hugh. I want to be with you" she said, her voice filled with sincerity.

Hugh's face lit up with a radiant smile, his eyes shimmering with happiness. He took Elizabeth's hand in his, their fingers intertwining. "I can't wait, Elizabeth," he whispered.

With their hearts aligned, Elizabeth and Hugh embraced the newfound love that blossomed between them, ready to embark on a journey that would intertwine their lives and forge a deep, unbreakable bond.

THE END

Printed in Great Britain
by Amazon

23549251R00303